ART
ETHON
THE EAGLE
and the
JAGUAR

A.P BESWICK

ACKNOWLEDGMENTS

To Rachel, Fran, Serene, Quinn and Neil. This book would not exist if not for your support and encouragement. To Victoria who continues to help me down this path.

CHAPTER 1

The sun beat down on the boy as he swung a large wooden stick against the old oak tree just outside his hut. He was practicing the latest training moves, but the heat was almost unbearable. His hair was matted with sweat and his clothes were wet from over-exertion. The shade cast by the old oak offered only slight comfort and while he was surrounded by grasslands and occasional trees, an unnatural, sinister haze sat over the landscape.

But he couldn't stop. He knew the consequences if he wasn't prepared and he didn't want to spend any more time locked inside the wooden hut. Not after last time, when he was stuck in there for six long days. He shuddered at the memory.

As he continued beating the weapon against the tree, his small hands began to blister. His skill was improving and his confidence was growing, but the sharp, uncomfortable sting in his palms finally made him pause to check the damage.

He sat on a large boulder and gasped. The sun had been warming the rock all morning and now it scalded the flesh on the back of his legs. He didn't flinch though. Pain didn't affect him as much as it used to. He had become accustomed to it, further punishment for not completing the tasks demanded of him.

He took a sip of water. It was warm, but still refreshing against his dry, cracked lips. The throbbing in his hands increased and he stared down at them. The blisters had all burst, leaving small flaps of white skin where the fluid inside had escaped. The pain was almost bearable, but that would change if they got infected. Reluctantly he dragged himself back to his hut to clean them.

Sweat dripped off him as he walked. It was getting even hotter and the boy looked forward to being inside and escaping the intensity of the blazing sun. But when he opened the door to the hut, he was greeted by a wall of stale, sticky air. He didn't know which was worse, being outside as his skin blistered in the sun, or sitting in the hut where the heat was less intense, yet the claustrophobic space made it harder to breathe.

As he crossed the room, the floor creaked. When he got to the sink, the tap was stuck and he had to apply extra force to release the much-needed water. Finally a slow trickle dripped into the basin and he groaned. His water supply was running low, so he would have to make the arduous mile-long journey to the river to refill the tank behind the hut.

The water stopped running when there was only a tiny amount in the sink and he had to choose between saving it to drink, or cleaning his hand. Wanting to avoid a painful infection, he placed his hand in the basin, watching as the water turned crimson from his blood. The throbbing got worse and he gritted his teeth. It stung like hell.

When he could bear it no longer, he wrapped his hand in a small towel and applied pressure. For just a moment he wished someone was with him, that someone could help him, rather than having to figure everything out on his own. He was far too young to be left alone to look after himself, yet through necessity he had become used to it.

Occasionally he was visited by a woman, but he did not look forward to these visits. They usually ended badly, with some form of punishment and the thought sent a shudder down his spine.

Hearing something outside, he panicked. *It's here, why so soon?*

He considered running, but there was only one door out of the hut and it would see him.

His heart raced with fear. *Why would it be back so soon? What does it want?*

His thoughts went into overdrive and his body flicked into fight or flight mode. He hated feeling like this. He hated her visiting. And more than anything he wanted to be ready so that one day he could fight her off and be free from this life.

The heavy breathing and grunting from the creature as it gathered itself from its landing was unmistakable. A shadow moved outside, coming ever closer and he could tell from the set of the wings that it was going to hurt him. His heart thumped, adrenaline shooting through him and his body trembled from the terror that was consuming him. His panic increased along with his dizziness and the room began to spin. Closing his eyes, he tried to steady himself, to focus, but the spinning and swirling inside his head just got worse.

With a cry of pain, he crashed to the floor.

The landing hurt, but it was not what he expected. Instead of hitting the wooden floor of the hut, the ground was earthy. He could taste dirt in the air around him. Opening his eyes, he saw the orange of the sun above him, even hotter than he was used to.

How am I outside?

His eyes stung, nausea made him heave and his head felt like it had been split open, such was the force of his headache. He touched his hand to his head just to make sure he had not cut himself from the fall, then dread consumed him again.

Where is it?

He jumped to his feet to look for the beast, but it was nowhere to be seen. Nor was his hut. Shocked, he surveyed the landscape. The large area of grasslands where he had spent his life had vanished, replaced with a busy, bustling market street. Stranger still, the haze had disappeared, making everything bright and clear. The air was breathable and the boy sucked in large gulps of it.

The biggest surprise was the people. He was no longer alone! As he walked down the busy street, people jostled against him and knocked him from side to side and he had to steady himself so he didn't fall. The closeness and the noise was overloading his senses and the smell of spices made him hungry. He looked over at one stand, where someone was selling strange powders, of multiple colours and fragrances.

"What are these?" he asked the man, whose skin was so much darker than his and the woman's.

"Kadam ladka!" the man replied, looking irate and gesturing wildly for him to move away.

Not understanding his words, but aware of the body language, the boy hastily left, worried he'd get a clout if he hung around.

He was amazed by everything around him, the people, the smells, the sounds. It was so different from what he was used to and he knew already that he liked this place so much more than where he lived. He didn't care what happened to him, he was just happy to be away and safe.

Still feeling disorientated, he continued down the street. With his pale skin and threadbare clothes, he stood out like a sore thumb amongst the people hustling and bustling around him. They were talking loudly over the stalls to each other, verging on shouting. He saw a stall with three chickens strung up, another with strange vegetables. Distracted, he bumped into someone and lost his footing, then another person walked into him and he was falling to the ground, the gravel stinging his already injured hands.

He tried to stand up amongst the sea of legs surrounding him, but was knocked down again. Desperately he crawled forward, looking for a gap to escape through. People walking past kicked him and nobody offered to help him, so maybe this place was no different to his after all.

Finally spotting a slight opening, he crawled as fast as he could towards it and found himself in an alleyway. Rolling onto his back, he gasped for air, then promptly turned over to spit out the dust he had just inhaled.

A slight breeze on the back of his neck refreshed him, but it was warm and gusting in short intervals. It wasn't a natural wind. Freezing with dread, he contemplated running, then opted to turn around and face whatever was breathing down his back.

"Mooo!" The loud noise from the cow startled him and he jumped backwards. He had seen plenty of cows before, but never one as mesmerising as this. It had no glow around it. He watched as it blinked its long eyelashes to keep the flies off. The boy reached out a hand to it, but the cow butted him, rejecting his advances, then moved towards him, pressing its large frame against him and pushing him backwards.

Seeing a market stall and a merchant behind him, the boy panicked, not wanting to crash into them. His heart raced and his head throbbed again and the same dizziness from earlier hit him like a sledgehammer. He shut his eyes to stop his surroundings spinning, then slammed to the ground.

This time he landed on a decrepit wooden floor. He was back in his wooden hut.

"Where have you been?"

The soft voice behind him made the hairs on his arms stand on end. How would she react to him vanishing, then reappearing in front of them. He had no idea where he had been, or how, but it was completely different from the world he lived in. And he knew he had to get back there somehow to escape this life.

"It's rude to not answer." She spoke with the same soft tone, but the boy knew the menacing undertone.

"I don't know," he replied, his voice trembling. Reluctantly dragging himself to his feet to face her, a wave of dizziness swamped him and he quickly sat down on a small stool.

"Did I say you could sit down? Who do you think you are?" she demanded, her voice becoming more assertive, more hostile.

Quickly the boy stood back up and looked at the floor, hoping not to make eye contact. "I'm s –"

Before he could say the word, he was struck across the face, hard. He flew across the room, his feet off the floor and slammed into the wall. The impact was terrible. The pain in his side was almost bearable, but the searing agony across his face was not.

It was like nothing he'd ever felt before. His face was on fire. Blood dripped onto the floor from the gaping wound. Woozily he looked up, to see the beast that struck him dissipating back towards the young woman who stood before him.

"Sorry mam!" he cried, reeling with shock. She had always been cold with him and at times cruel, but she had never been this aggressive and he was scared about what might happen next.

His mum walked slowly past him and brushed his blood-soaked, matted hair from his eyes. "That's going to leave a nasty scar boy," she teased, the chill in her voice sharp and icy. "Now you are going to try really hard to get back to where you've been and while there you will find a way to bring me back with you."

Bending forward, she kissed the boy on the head. Blood stained her bottom lip and she smiled a terrible smile. "You wouldn't want me to get angry again." And she turned and swept out of the hut.

The boy crumpled to the floor and curled up in a ball.

Crying into his chest, his face burned like molten metal had been poured on it.

He needed to find a way to save himself. He needed to find a way to escape this hell.

He needed to get back to wherever it was he had just been.

CHAPTER 2

Staring into his phone, Arnold dialled the number with little hope that his friend would answer. After all, he hadn't spoken to him all summer. He waited patiently as the phone continued to ring out.

"Hey, you're through to Otto. Leave a message and I will get back to you." Arnold had become so used to the voice message having lost count of how many times he had tried ringing, each time hoping that Otto would just pick up the phone and speak to him.

He sighed as the phone bleeped, indicating that he could now leave a message. "Otto, it's me again. It's getting kind of difficult to keep talking to your voicemail. Hope you are doing ok, ring me back if you get this" He ended the call and placed it against his forehead, tapping it as he thought about everything that had happened just a couple of months ago.

Everett returned into the room and sat next to Arnold placing her head on his shoulder. "Did he answer?" she asked, knowing what the response would be.

"Nope," Arnold replied, resting his head back against Everett and taking hold of her hand. "I hope he's ok."

"He's away with his dad. He will be fine. I'm sure he will

catch up with you when he gets back." Everett was unaware that Otto had been expelled from the Chichen for taking a life. Arnold had not shared this information with her, not feeling that people would understand Otto's reason. He fully believed that Otto would have had no choice to do what he had done following Sue's betrayal.

Otto's dad had gone ballistic at Arthur, following his son's expulsion from the Chichen. Even though it was the head of the Chichen, Mr. Whittaker, who had made the decision that led to his removal. Otto's dad had fumed to Arthur that his family's honour had been cast into doubt. He blamed him for not protecting his son. The day after this confrontation, Otto had left the town with his dad but no one knew where they had gone or what they were doing.

"I hope so. I didn't leave things in a good place the last time I saw him." Arnold was referring to the night that he was kidnapped and the night his grandad was murdered.

Arnold had spent the whole summer with Everett and George. They had helped keep him grounded since his grandad had been taken away from him. He had been consumed by grief in the aftermath of the night at the tower and had thrown himself into his training, the result of which had now left him feeling and looking much fitter. He had grown into his frame more and had more of a physical presence than he had had last year. He felt as though his senses had become stronger. The training he had put himself through as well as Everett and George's company had kept him busy. However, deep down, Arnold knew that this was a distraction. He knew that he'd not fully grieved for his grandad or gained the closure that he needed.

There was one more week to go before they would be back at school and Arnold was not looking forward to it. In the aftermath of his grandad's murder, the media attention had been intrusive, not helped by the Chichen's reluctance to give the hungry journalists any information about Levent. He was told this was to stop a widespread panic about the link to the spirit world, but Arnold was not stupid and he did not fully believe them. He felt that everyone should know what happened and he hated keeping it a secret. The only people he had confided in were Everett and George who he had sworn to secrecy about what really happened at the tower. However, he hadn't shared with them the true reason Otto had expelled from the Chichen.

Everett sat up straight next to Arnold, the sun catching her hair. Arnold admired her prettiness. He felt fortunate to have her sat with him in his room and even luckier to be able to call her his girlfriend. "School is next week. So I'm sure he will be there. You will be able to speak to him then and clear things up."

"I hope so," he replied. All he wanted was to make amends with his closest friend.

"Right - enough moping! It's beautiful outside and I want an ice cream from the parlour. Let's go there and then we can come up with a plan for today. I don't want to sit around doing nothing." There was an assertive manner to Everett's comments which made Arnold realise that he had had about as much sympathy as he was going to get from her for one day.

Realising that it was a pointless exercise to disagree with her, he stood up and stretched before smiling at Everett. "Come on then. It's too hot to stay here."

Leaving the house, Arnold enjoyed the warmth of the bright morning sun against his skin. The street was filled with children enjoying their last week of freedom before the start of the new term. Two doors down from Arnold's house, four girls were throwing a football from one side of the street to the other, attempting to hit the kerb on the opposite side. Stopping momentarily, one of them shouted "Car!" and the four of them stopped what they were doing to let the vehicle pass before resuming their game. There were other children in the garden opposite his house screaming with joy. Arnold smiled as he saw Brandon chasing his big sister around with a hosepipe, taking their water fight to a new level.

"I used to love Kerby," Everett recalled. "I always beat George when we played." Arnold wasn't surprised at all as Everett was by far the more competitive. They locked hands and began to walk down the street towards the ice cream parlour, which was just a short walk from Arnolds's house. Arnold could feel a bead of sweat forming on his forehead due to the heat and by the time they had got there, he was more than ready to get an ice cream to cool himself down. Looking into the sizeable fridge in front of him, he began to mull over the vast choice of ice cream that lay before him.

"What do you fancy?" he asked, wanting Everett to choose first before he made his choice.

"I think I will go for the strawberry and cream, please," pressing her finger against the glass to point out her selection.

"Mint choc chip for me please, in a waffle cone," he followed.

The lady behind the counter gave the two of them a smile before preparing their chosen ice creams for them. They left the parlour and crossed the road, sitting at the pavilion in the centre of town which sat opposite the cenotaph. The cenotaph was a tribute to locals that had died during the second world war. A bronze statue of a soldier running holding a rifle sat in the centre, with an angel stood over the top looking over him. The statue rightfully took centre stage in the town and it was a beautiful tribute to those that had made the ultimate sacrifice. The two of them sat for a moment, enjoying the instant satisfaction that the cold ice cream brought them from the relentless heat.

Looking down the road, Arnold wondered what Everett might want to do next. Still, he was quickly distracted as he saw something moving towards him that he instantly recognised. It was a white Ford C-Max with blacked-out windows at the rear and he knew exactly whose car it was.

"That's Otto's dad's car!" He stood up, excited at what this meant; his best friend was home.

"Are you sure?" Everett quizzed, standing just behind

him.

Arnold had focused in on the number plate, courtesy of his enhanced vision. The car turned and knowing the route like the back of his hand, Arnold knew that they were driving to their house.

"We need to go." Arnold threw his ice cream to the side and began running, wanting to get to Otto's house as fast as he could.

"Wait!" Everett called, but her attempts to stop him fell on deaf ears.

Arnold continued to run down the street, his thoughts swirling around his head. He had so many things he wanted to speak to him about but most of all, he just wanted to make sure that Otto was ok. Continuing his steady pace, he ran through the streets until eventually, he reached Otto's house. Outside sat the white C-Max that had passed them just a few minutes before. Arnold stopped running, allowing his breath to catch him up. He felt fitter than he had previously, however, he was dripping with sweat from the exertion and the weather.

Once his breathing had slowed, he stepped forward to the front door and knocked using the lion head door knocker. Three short knocks were followed by a long pause. Arnold waited patiently, looking at the frosting at the top of the door to change colour, a quick indication if someone was going to open the door. A few more moments passed and there was no answer, so he knocked again, this time hearing footsteps coming towards the front door. There was muffled shouting behind the door and then suddenly it swung open. Stood there was Mr. Redburn, who was wearing his suit pants and a blue shirt with the sleeves rolled up to his elbows. His dark amber eyes, a tinge of green identical to Otto's stared intently at Arnold.

"You are not welcome here. Leave!" He was short and direct, which was typical of his manner given that he was town mayor and needed to be ruthless at times.

"I just want to speak with Otto, please," Arnold replied,

hoping that the conversation would swing in a different direction.

"He doesn't want to see you." Mr. Redburn was curt and straight to the point, an air of frustration in his tone.

"If I could just-" Mr. Redburn cut him off once more.

"Don't you think you have done enough damage? Otto's expulsion is all your fault! What's happened is on you!" Behind him, the vestibule door opened to reveal a much smaller person. It was Otto's little brother, Adan.

"Nold, Nold!" he exclaimed, flapping his hands with excitement and pushing past Mr. Redburn to greet Arnold at the front door. Adan had always referred to him as Nold, as he couldn't quite manage Arnold due to his autism-related communication difficulties. Arnold felt happy to see him too and crouched down to his level and smiled at him. "Wow, you have grown," he said, speaking gently and slowly, allowing Adan time to process what he said. Adan avoided eye contact but gave Arnold a huge smile indicating that he had understood what he had said to him.

"Come inside, Adan." Mr. Redburn placed his hand on him and attempted to manoeuvre him back inside." Adan shrugged off his hand and let out a loud shout in disapproval.

"Nold, Nold," he said, tugging on Arnold's t-shirt, unable to understand why he was not coming in.

"It's ok, buddy," Arnold said gently, realising that Adan was beginning to show signs of distress. "Listen to your dad." He gave the boy a smile and stood back up.

Adan turned and walked back inside, allowing Mr. Redburn to stand alone at the front of the door. "Don't come back here again. You have no idea, what you have done to this family!" Mr. Redburn stepped back inside and before Arnold had the chance to say another word. He had slammed the door shut, the door rattling in its frame. A couple walking their dog on the other side of the street turned their heads to see what was happening.

Deflated, he began to walk back towards where he had

left Everett, he could feel his frustration building up. He understood Mr. Redburn was annoyed at Otto being thrown out of the Chichen, but that had nothing to do with him. He had no say whatsoever in the final decision and his dad had fought for Otto to be allowed to carry on his training. Unable to understand why Otto's Dad was taking his frustrations out on him, Arnold kicked a stone against a wall as he continued his journey back to the centre of town. In the distance, he could see Everett sat on the bench where he had left her, except now she had company.

Focusing closely, he could see that she had been joined by Peter, a boy from school. Peter raised his hand and brushed his hand through Everett's hair, who in turn, pushed it away and looked annoyed. Arnold felt his blood boil and he set off running towards the two of them.

"Oi!" he shouted, "Keep your hands to yourself." Peter stood up from the bench and grinned at Arnold, his smug smile infuriating Arnold even further. Arnold hated this boy, who, in his eyes, got away with doing whatever he wanted. All because his parents had money and they backed him come what may. He could never do any wrong in their eyes and it meant that Peter walked around like he was untouchable.

"What are you gonna do?" He goaded as Arnold drew level with the two of them.

"Excuse me?" Everett interjected, standing up from her seat and looking unimpressed with the two of them metaphorically beating their chests like a couple of wild gorillas. "I'm perfectly capable of looking after myself, thank you." She looked directly at Arnold and he knew he was in for it straight away. He stood staring at Peter, wanting to wipe the smirk from his face. Knowing what the consequences would be, he raised his hands up, indicating that nothing further was going to happen.

"That's right Ethon, let this cow stick up for you again. You are pathetic," Peter sneered, trying to get a reaction from him. Everett turned from Arnold and swung her arm out, punching Peter straight in the nose. He whimpered as he fell backwards. Arnold felt the crunch of the impact and couldn't help but smile.

"That is for putting your hands on me without me saying it was ok to do so." She walked up to Peter, who was on his knees, cradling his nose that had begun to bleed. "Lesson learned?" Peter fell to his side, letting out another groan as the discomfort from the blow set in. She spun back towards Arnold and then walked past him, smirking to herself. Arnold turned to follow her.

"Everett, that was amazing." He smiled at how she had put Peter in his place.

"That has been a long time coming," she replied, shaking her hand at the discomfort from the blow. Her smile showing that it was worth it. "I had best get some ice for this." Everett winced, "Walk me to mine?" Arnold nodded and the two of them walked to Everett's house.

"My mum is going to flip," Everett moaned, bracing herself as she opened the front door. She turned to face Arnold. "She hates that I am not a girly girl like she wants me to be."

"I think you're pretty great the way you are." Arnold felt the familiar redness reach his cheeks. He wanted to kick himself for how cheesy his words sounded.

"Aww, cute." Leaning forward, she gave him a quick kiss goodbye. "I'll text you later," she smiled, as she shut the door.

Arnold was on cloud nine and the scuffle that had just taken place had distracted him from how rude Mr. Redburn had been to him. He walked back through town, not paying attention to what was going on around him, simply thinking about Everett and how happy he was that he had here as his girlfriend.

A short time later, Arnold had just reached his front door where he was greeted by his dad. He looked flustered and was pacing back and forth in the living room.

"It's ok, Arthur." His mum was attempting to calm him

down, but it was not working.

"No, it's not, it's gone, everything has gone!" he ranted, as he paced the room. He stopped when he saw that Arnold had arrived home.

"What's happened? What's gone?" Arnold asked, a puzzled look etched across his face.

"There has been a break-in at your grandad's house," his mum answered, her soft and soothing voice attempting to encourage calm.

"What?" Arnold felt taken aback. He hadn't been to his grandad's house since he had died. He had not been ready.

"Everything from the attic is gone. There isn't any damage – it's all just gone." His dad was irate. "We only went up to sort through your Grandad's clothes and realised straight away that someone had been inside. They knew exactly what they wanted too. Nothing else has been taken." Arnold didn't know what to say. There was lots of old-looking stuff up there, but Arnold didn't feel that there had been anything sentimental. Opting to keep out of the way, Arnold went up to his bedroom wondering where the contents of his grandad's loft had gone and why someone would take them. What's more, how had they gotten in so easily?

CHAPTER 3

The next morning, Arnold sat at the dining table eating some cereal. He had already heard his dad explaining to his mum that he was unable to notify the Doyens of the break-in as they would ask about what had been taken. Arnold was aware that he had been hiding artefacts up there from when he was an Elder and the Doyens would not be happy.

The newspaper lay on the table, having been delivered by the over-eager paperboy who Arnold thought started his round far too early. He was sure that he had heard the letterbox just after six o'clock this morning and the metal shutter slamming shut was just loud enough to disturb him from his sleep. This meant that Arnold was feeling a little bit grumpy as he made his way through his breakfast.

Picking up the paper, he first looked at the back page to see whether Everton had made any movements in the transfer market but apart from a couple of players he had never heard of there didn't seem to be much going on. He spun the paper around to look at the front and was taken aback by what he read. In bright, bold letters the heading shouted, "Menial Uprising". His interest spiked by the headline, Arnold began to read the article underneath and discovered that a spike in crimes by menials have been reported over the last four weeks. What is a menial?

Arnold couldn't help but feel this had something to do with Levent. After all, he had proudly announced that he had people everywhere. Pausing for a moment, Arnold wondered if he would show up again. The fear of another confrontation is what had motivated him to train harder. He wanted to come face to face with Levent, but only when he was ready and able to avenge his grandad's death. His dad walked into the room, finishing his toast before turning to leave.

"Have you seen this?" Arnold asked.

His dad nodded, looking harassed following the break-in at his grandad's house. "I'm working on it at the moment. When Levent appears again I want to make sure we are ready for him. It has to be linked with your grandad's house being burgled." His dad clearly had a plan somewhat similar to Arnold's own. Turning on his heels, his dad left the room to leave for work. Since his grandad's death his dad had been starting work early and finishing late.

Hearing the door shut, Arnold picked up the Oswald advertiser once more to read more of the front-page story.

"I'm off to work now." His mum poked her head through the door. "Can you hoover up for me, please?"

"No problem," he answered without lifting his head from the newspaper. He heard the door shut again and continued with his breakfast before going back upstairs to get dressed for the day. When Arnold came back downstairs, he noticed that there was a letter sat on the mat by the front door. Arnold felt this strange as the postman didn't usually arrive until the afternoon. Arnold stepped forward picking up the envelope from the floor, the hard bristles from the doormat pressing against his hand. He turned the envelope over to see that it simply said 'Arnold' in the centre. The handwriting was old fashioned and intricate, like calligraphy.

Realising that the post had been hand-delivered, he quickly opened up the front door to look outside, but he could not see anyone around. Still stood at the doorway, he ran his finger inside the top, breaking the seal to see what was inside.

Opening the envelope revealed a small piece of card. Arnold removed it and read the message that was written in the same style of writing that was on the front of the envelope.

'Bramley Lockup, number 127 – Do not share this with the Chichen.'

He knew that Bramley Lockup was on the far side of town, but Arnold felt slightly confused by what it meant. Normally, he would have instantly contacted Otto for his opinion, but this was not currently an option for him, so he took out his phone and dialled Everett's number to see what she thought. The phone rang out without being answered so Arnold decided to call round to her house and ask her in person. Grabbing his things, he locked his front door and set off to Everett's house. A short walk later and he arrived outside Everett's, Arnold walked up the short path before knocking on the door with some urgency.

A few moments later the door opened to reveal a bleary-eyed George, her white bunny pyjamas indicating that she'd had a sleepover at Everett's. She yawned and rubbed her hand on the back of her matted red hair. "Dude, what time do you call this?" She was clearly unimpressed at the unnaturally early time that he had called round.

"It's half ten", Arnold replied. He knew that Everett and George liked to lie in with it usually being the afternoon before they would meet up. "I need you two to see this."

"Hey." Everett popped her head on George's shoulder. "You're keen this morning." Arnold began to blush as Everett was stood in her pink nightdress, something he hadn't seen before.

"Sorry," he began to bumble. "This was just posted through my door and wanted to see what you thought." Passing her the card, she read it and then passed it to George. "What do you think?" He pressed them for an answer; he trusted them both and would welcome a second and third opinion.

"We need to go to this address and check it out," Everett announced. "Give us an hour to get ready and then we will head over," she said eagerly.

"Woah, we can't just head straight there! What if it is a trap? What if it's Levent?" George asked, being the more cautious of the three. "It's potentially dangerous, Arnold. You need to tell your dad."

"It clearly says not to let the Chichen know, George and my dad is a Doyen," Arnold said. "It's why I came here and nowhere else."

"Safety in numbers. There are three of us," Everett said, making the decision on Arnold's behalf. George sighed, accepting defeat in the discussion.

"Fine. Give us an hour." She turned and headed up the stairs to get herself ready.

"Meet us at the cenotaph at half eleven," Everett said, stepping down from the doorway and kissing Arnold on the cheek before running back inside, shutting the door behind her.

Arnold headed straight to the cenotaph as directed and sat on a bench. He pulled out his phone to check his social media and play a game as he waited for the girls to arrive. The weather was slightly overcast with the clouds blocking out the sun and there was a faint musk in the air which indicated that the local farmers had been out muck spreading. After checking his social media once more, Arnold placed his phone back in his pocket and sat looking down the road. He was beginning to feel bored with waiting. He did contemplate going to the address by himself but decided it was not worth the roasting he would receive from Everett if he did.

Gazing across the road, he suddenly saw Otto walking past carrying a brown bag in front of him. Arnold couldn't help but notice that he looked bigger as if he had been working out a lot. His light blue vest revealed toned arms and Arnold was taken aback by how much Otto had changed. Realising this was his chance to talk to him, he bellowed across the road trying to get his attention. "Otto!" Arnold called out, waving his arms in an attempt to attract his attention. Glancing over, Otto made eye contact then turned his head back, choosing to ignore Arnold and carry on with his journey. His body language was nervous; he seemed as though he didn't want to be out in town at all and the speed Otto was walking implied that he wanted to get home as fast as he could. Arnold felt frustrated at how his old friend had just blanked him and shouted again. Otto continued on his path and around the corner until he was then out of sight. Arnold contemplated running after him but realised it would be a complete waste of time. He needed to remain focused on going to the address he had received on the card he had received this morning.

He waited patiently until eventually Everett and George appeared, ready to walk down to the Bramley lock-up and see what all the fuss was about. "I have just seen Otto," Arnold told them as soon as the two of them reached him.

"How was he?" George asked.

"Ignorant and bigger." Arnold talked through how Otto had blanked him and rushed off and that he looked as though he had been working out a lot while he had been away.

"Looking forward to seeing him even more now," George teased, playfully.

"He seemed really distracted. I am worried about him," Arnold said, ignoring her.

"It must have hit him hard being kicked out of the Chichen for failing a test, especially when he was doing so well," Everett suggested.

This was the only way Arnold had thought he could explain Otto being kicked out of the Chichen. Not wanting to share that he had actually taken a life in self-defence which in turn had broken a fundamental rule. He didn't want them to judge a situation they were not involved in and he did not want them to look at Otto any differently.

Arnold didn't know how to reply, instead choosing to awkwardly switch the topic of the conversation back to getting up to the Bramley lock up. "We can come up with a plan about Otto later, we need to head up to the lock-up."

The three of them set off up the main road knowing that the lock-up was not too far away. They reached the bottom of the main road before taking a left turn, walking past the old hobbit holes and into an industrial estate that looked as though it had seen better days. On their right were some garages set up with a wide range of old cars littering the dusty grounds in front of them. The garages did not look as if they were maintained well, the layout of them looking messy from the outside. The mechanics could be heard laughing and joking with each other and the sound of air guns being used to remove the bolts out of a wheel filled the air. "I wouldn't want them sorting my car out," Everett quipped as they walked past, the dust from the ground leaving a small cloud around them as they walked up the road.

"You don't drive," George laughed "and with your temperament, I would not like to be in a car with you when you do start lessons!"

"Harsh, too harsh," Everett replied, playfully kicking a stone and skimming it across the floor until it clattered against the metal fencing in front of them. The noise drew the attention of the mechanics from the garage who looked over at them. The three of them began laughing and chuckling to each other as the continued up the road towards the Bramley lock up.

Turning the corner, they saw the lock-up just off the path. It looked as equally unkempt as the garages that they had just passed. The building was a single storey and the worn stone front was littered with graffiti. A single pane of glass to the side of the door revealed an old vending machine that Arnold couldn't help but feel contained out of date chocolates.

"Is it even open?" George wondered aloud.

"It looks derelict," Arnold added.

"Are you sure this is the place?" Everett put her face against the window, using her hand to brush the window before squinting, trying to look through the dirty window.

"Er, given the sign there, I would say this is the right place." George pointed to a broken sign that had Bramley painted on it. "If I didn't feel this was a trap before I definitely do now. No one is here." Undeterred, Arnold reached forward to the door handle and pressed against it; the door was locked. Everett and George looked across at him.

"It was worth a try," he said, shrugging. "We should look around the back," he continued and he began to lead the way, with Everett and George following behind him.

"Did you not hear what I just said? This is definitely a trap!" George's protest fell on deaf ears as Arnold continued to walk around to the rear of the building, desperate to know what – or who - he had been brought here to see. Reaching the back of the building, they could see the grounds behind the building were surrounded by a tall. Stone wall.

"Need a boost over?" Arnold smiled, as he stood with his back against the wall placing his hands on his knee to offer Everett a lift. Looking unimpressed with this gesture, Everett ran at the section of the wall beside Arnold, using one foot to run up the wall before grabbing the ledge and pulling herself up and sitting on top, looking down on Arnold and George.

Arnold laughed to himself. He didn't know why he bothered asking really. He looked at George and indicated for her to use his boost to get up the wall. "You next."

"I think I will wait here and stand guard. I feel really uncomfortable about this," George said nervously.

"We can't leave you here," Arnold said, "We need to stay together."

"I will wait around the front on the road. If you guys

don't message me every ten minutes, I will call for help."
She paused. "I really don't have a good feeling about this."

"Are you sure?" Everett wasn't happy about leaving her
best friend behind.

"I'll be fine. If anyone comes around, I will ring you."
George stepped back and straightened her beanie hat before
heading back to the front of the building.

Arnold stepped away from the wall to give himself a
good start at scaling it, praying that he managed it first time
as Everett would mock him for the rest of the day if he
didn't. Running at the wall, he managed to push off against
it and pull himself up, going one step further than Everett
and vaulting straight over the top, landing on the overgrown
ground on the opposite side.

"Show off." Everett grinned as she hopped off the wall,
landing on her feet next to Arnold. "Where now?"

The grounds were extensive with multiple storage crates
scattered across the courtyard. The various colours of the
rusted containers brought some colour to the overgrown
landscape. "What number was it?"

"127," Arnold replied, creeping around one of the crates
as he attempted to ascertain whether or not they were
numbered. "This one says number forty-three," he said,
pointing to the number that had been etched onto the side
of the crate. "It must be towards the bottom of the yard."

Everett and Arnold began wandering through the
overgrown grass that had taken over. There were weeds,
plants and grass growing everywhere throughout the
courtyard, giving it a dystopian feel. They made their way
through and eventually reached the top of the yard. "Just let
me message George." Everett took out her phone and sent
a quick message to her to let her know they were ok. George
replied with a smiley face emoji complete with a beanie hat
on top.

The two of them continued to look around the crates
but were unable to locate the one that they were looking for.
They followed a row of containers until they reached the

bottom.

"Strange," Arnold said, confusion covering his face.

"What?"

"The last storage crate here is 126." Arnold stepped back to look at where they had just walked. The crates on the row they had walked down were numbered in order. Stepping around the side of the last crate, they could see another container on its own, hidden behind the others. "This must be it," Arnold said, frowning at it. "It looks different though." Walking over to it, he could see that the crate was sat by itself, the grass and vines around it creeping up the sides. "I can't see anyone around."

"Strange. Well, let's not wait around all day. We need to check it out," said Everett, who had decided to take control of the situation. She strode ahead to the front of the crate, wanting to get a better look. "Come on!" Arnold followed her, not wanting to fall too far behind. He stopped when he reached the front. "Now what?" he sighed.

"Wasn't there a key with your note?" Everett asked, beginning to look a little bit exasperated at the situation.

"Need a lock to use a key," Arnold said, pointing out that there did not appear to be any form of lock on the front of the crate, just a series of hieroglyphs denoting some animals. Looking at the last symbol, Arnold noticed that it was a picture of an elk. He looked more closely. "That's too much of a coincidence for me," he said.

"What is?" Everett replied while kicking some grass back away from the front of the overgrown crate.

Arnold pointed at the final hieroglyph denoting an elk. "That was my grandad's spirit beast."

"That is a coincidence and given everything that has gone on recently, I don't really do coincidences." Everett stepped back from the crate, raising her hand to look at her watch. She realised ten more minutes had passed and she needed to contact George. Taking out her phone, she messaged to let her know that the two of them were safe.

The two of them continued to stare at the front of the

storage crate, wondering what to do next. Everett took her phone out of her pocket, looking at it with a worried look on her face.

"What's wrong?" Arnold asked while pushing against the front of the crate in the hope that it would dislodge and they would be able to get in.

"She hasn't messaged me back."

"Try ringing her, she probably hasn't noticed the message," Arnold suggested, continuing to examine the crate for ways to gain entry. Everett pressed George's picture on her phone and it began to ring out.

"She's not answering, we're going to have to turn back to check on her. I'll kill her if she has her phone on silent again." Everett was about to hang up when the call connected.

"Where have you been?" Everett snapped.

George didn't speak.

"Are you there, George? What are you doing?" Everett listened for a reply, but there wasn't one. The silence on the line was interrupted by a low growling noise, followed by a loud scream. "George!" Everett screamed, the colour draining from her face. She stared in horror at Arnold. "It's him!"

Arnold's heart began racing. He ran past Everett, grabbing her hand as he went past so they could get back to George. "Come on!" Arnold set off sprinting through the thick grass, wanting to get back as fast as he could. Everett let out a yelp as she crashed against the floor, catching her foot on a vine. Arnold spun to see what had happened and seeing Everett on the floor he stopped to go back and help her up.

"No!" she shouted, "Go help George!" Arnold nodded and spun back around, running back to the wall at speed. He hopped over the wall with ease. As Arnold landed, he could hear an aggressive growling noise. Arnold hoped that it was a guard dog and not Levent's remaining lion.

Sprinting around the corner, he saw George laid out on

the floor with something stood over her. Arnold focused on what it was but couldn't make it out. He was unable to use his enhanced vision from that distance. Arnold ran over and began to shout but as he got close. He soon realised the unmistakable glow around the creature which indicated that it was a spirit beast that was stood over her.

"George!" he yelled, trying to get the spirit beast's attention. This worked and it began to turn around to face him, letting a loud roar. *What the hell is that?* he wondered to himself. The creature then began to move from being on all fours to standing on two legs, the spectral glow around it appearing green and fierce like dancing flames. It began to run towards Arnold at pace, dropping back onto all fours and rapidly picking up speed.

Arnold began to move his hands until they began to illuminate a light blue colour. His hands becoming warm with the sensation, he could feel his spirit beast rising up from within him, his eagle bursting forward and flying up in the air above him before diving back down at the beast in front of him.   His eagle let out a shriek as it dive-bombed down to intercept the attack. The bright blue glow around it making it look fierce, intimidating and angelic all at the same time. Swooping down it clattered straight into the spectral beast which bounced onto its side, letting out a grunt as it crashed into the side of the Bramley lock-up. The dust engulfed the creature as again it stood on all fours, Arnold could see the shape of the beast but could not make out any of the finer details, apart from the bright green glowing eyes that shone brightly through the dust cloud. Another loud roar followed, this one borne of frustration and the creature moved backwards and ran away down the road.

Arnold ran to George, who still lay unmoving on the floor. The tracks around her showed she had been knocked over then dragged towards the side of the road. Arnold slid on the ground and dropped to his knees bringing himself to a stop as he made it level with her "George!" He pulled her up towards him and she let out a groan as he lifted her to a sitting position. "Thank god you're ok!" he said as he hugged her, his worry subsiding now that he knew that she wasn't severely injured.

"What happened?" George asked hesitantly as she gathered her bearings.

Arnold smiled at her "I was hoping you would tell me. Are you ok?"

"I think so. Where's Everett?" George quickly asked, worrying about her best friend.

Everett had just scaled the wall and could be heard running down the side of the building in their direction. Catching up to them, she looked petrified. "Oh my god!" she panted as she drew level with the two of them. "Where's Levent and his lion?"

"I have no idea as that wasn't either of them." Arnold stood up and helped to pull George back to her feet. "I have no idea what that was, but I have never seen anything like it." Arnold pulled out his phone.

"What are you doing?" Everett asked.

"I need to speak to my Dad. He might be able to help."

"But the note said not to let the Chichen know," Everett reminded him.

"George is ok, they don't need to know why I'm here. We can't hide what has happened." Arnold began to call his dad.

George dusted herself down and picked her beanie hat back up. She placed it back on her head, covering her dark red hair in the process, somehow managing to pack her head of tight curls inside it. "See I bloody told you it was a trap! Levent is up to something and I do not like it one bit," she said, her broad accent taking over her usual softly spoken demeanour, highlighting that she was not happy at Arnold and Everett for not listening to her.

"What was it?" Everett pressed, eager for more information.

"I have no idea, I only saw the spirit beast," Arnold

answered, the adrenaline still coursing through his veins.

"Well, what was that?" Everett continued to push.

"Again, I don't know," he responded, somewhat confused. "It stood up on its back legs and I don't know any spirit beasts that can do that. It can't have been Levent's lion."

"Are you sure?" George asked, continuing to dust herself down.

"Neither of his lions had bright green glowing eyes." Arnold's phone rang out as the call to his dad went unanswered. Everett walked across to George, giving her a warm embrace, relieved that she was ok. "Maybe it's a good thing he didn't answer," she shrugged.

"Er, what do you mean?" George was clearly unimpressed with Everett's statement. "Why wouldn't we let the Doyen's know?"

"No one was hurt. If we ring the Doyen's they are going to want to know what we were doing here and between the three of us, we will give it away easily. Remember the note said not to let the Doyens know. Everett was taking her usual assertive stance.

"She's right, George," Arnold said.

"Oh, what a surprise! You taking your girlfriend's side," George said sarcastically as she turned and began to walk away.

"Give me a few days," Arnold reasoned. "Let me see if we can get in that crate. If we can't, then I will tell my dad everything."

"And if that spirit beast turns up again?" George said, continuing to look unimpressed.

"Then we will let them know," Everett added. George paused for a moment while she considered what had been said.

"Fine." She crossed her arms as her form of rebellion against the others, not fully onside with their plan. "If anyone gets hurt though, that is on you."

Arnold looked at his phone once more, deciding not to

ring his dad and placing it back inside his jeans pocket. "I will head to the athenaeum and see if I can find anything that might help us get past that rune."

"Here's hoping that you do. We need to leave for the time being in case whatever that thing is comes back," George said as the three of them set off back towards town.

Arnold couldn't help but feel disturbed by the fact that George had seemingly been the target and not him. Surely if it was Levent, he would have attacked him directly? And if it wasn't Levent, whose spirit beast had they just encountered? The only thing he was sure of was that this spirit beast was not a lion. It was something else far more terrifying.

CHAPTER 4

Arnold slammed the thick book against the table he was sat at, the loud bang an indication of his growing frustration. The old, dusted and worn book was an ancient codex that was hidden within the walls of the Chichen. This codex contained explanations of every type of spirit beast known going back hundreds of years. It had drawings, descriptions and even sections on their identified strengths and weaknesses. Arnold had not found any information that resembled the spirit beast he had seen, especially the bright green glowing eyes. There was not a single description of a spirit beast with eyes like this so far. However, after the three days he had spent reading this codex, he still had nearly a quarter of it left to discover. Some pages were difficult to read due to the old-fashioned handwriting and some of the pictures were faded, but Arnold was able to decipher the majority of it. He remained hopeful that he would find something.

Arnold placed his hands against his face as he attempted to gather himself, knowing that he needed to continue to focus if he was to keep going. His eyes were tired and heavy from the constant reading and thinking about what had happened earlier that week. All that kept coming back to him were those haunting emerald green eyes and he knew that they were the key to figuring out what kind of spirit beast had attacked George.

The storage container had been at the back of his mind but this current task took priority. He knew that he would also need to research the symbol he saw on the container door, to look for ways of getting inside it. There had been no further reports of the spirit beast that they had encountered so, for now, Arnold had not spoken to his dad about it. He really didn't want the Chichen to know the real reason they were there. Arnold had no clue what was in that storage container; all they had to go off was the mysterious note that Arnold had received in the post earlier in the week, with no indication who it was from.

His phone beeped, indicating he had received a message. It was Everett, asking how he was getting on with his research. Arnold quickly typed out a message back, informing her that he had not found anything useful yet. Looking at the time on his phone, he realised it was getting late and he had best head home. Unfortunately for Arnold, he wasn't allowed to take this codex home with him due to its age and value which is what had restricted him to the confines of the athenaeum in the first place. He had been tempted to disregard this rule but with the memory of how firm they were on Otto being exiled from the Chichen fresh in his mind, Arnold did not want to risk it. After all, he still wanted to be a Doyen one day. He walked across to the side of the room where row upon row of codex lay, tightly compacted into their bookshelves. He placed the book back into the shelf and then walked back across the room to exit and head home.

As he was walking over the to the opaque glass double doors they unfrosted before opening, Mr. Whitaker walked in, alongside his dad.

"I've noticed you have been spending quite a lot of time in here the last few days and not the training room." Mr. Whittaker began with his well-spoken tone not fitting in with everyone else's broader Lancashire accents.

"Just fancied doing some reading sir," Arnold replied, not wanting to give anything away.

"Let's hope that's all it is," he replied, clearly not believing what Arnold was saying to him. Arnold had taken an even greater dislike to Mr. Whittaker as he had been the one with the final say on Otto and his brief time at the Chichen. His relationship with him was strained, but his dad had explained to him that whatever his emotions were towards Mr. Whittaker, Arnold needed to grin and bear it as he was the Elder and he needed to respect that.

Taking this into account, Arnold returned a smile to Mr. Whittaker before replying "Just having a break from the physical training. Dad told me to rest as he thought I had been overdoing it."

"Is this true, Arthur?" Mr. Whittaker asked Arnold's dad. Arthur looked at Arnold in disapproval of the situation that his son had just placed him in.

"I did sir," he responded instinctively.

"Very well, if you insist. Ethon, we need this room for a meeting. Please can you vacate - there are other rooms available and if you wish to use them, that is fine. Given that you are resting may I suggest that you call it a night and return home?" He spoke with a sarcastic tone, a clear indication to Arnold that he was suspicious of him. Arnold began to leave the room, nodding to his dad as he walked past. He couldn't help but smirk once he had passed the pair and he walked through the double doors to head towards the exit.

As he left the Chichen, he waved at the new receptionist, Grace. She smiled back at Arnold as she typed away on the desktop computer that sat in front of her. Grace had been at the Chichen for around a month now. Following Sue's betrayal, the Chichen decided that anybody coming to work for them had to demonstrate that they possessed a spirit beast. Grace seemed like a nice lady; she was in her fifties with short grey hair and glasses that looked like they were too large for her face. The truth was, Arnold felt very guarded after what Sue had done; she had been allowed to get into the Chichen, get close to everyone and kidnap him for Levent. Levent had told him that he had people everywhere and those words had remained in the back of his mind all summer, even more so after George was attacked by the unknown spirit beast.

He left the Chichen but rather than heading home, he had a sudden change of plan. The thoughts of Levent being back made him feel like he needed to be more proactive in being ready for him. He turned and headed back up to the outskirts of town, towards the Bramley lockup. He wanted to check container 127 once more before he headed home. Tomorrow he was back to school, then after school he was at the Chichen so it would be at least next weekend before he would be able to return. It was evening and although it was cooler than it had been earlier in the day, there was still a stickiness in the air.

Before long, Arnold found himself walking through the overgrown grounds of the Bramley lockup, making his way to the far side of the courtyard to where storage container 127 stood. He could hear the telling off he would get from Everett and George when they found out that he had come here by himself. It wasn't the brightest thing he had ever done, but he felt more than able to defend himself if that spirit beast was to return. He approached the front of the storage container again looking at the front of it from all angles just in case there was some form of a switch for him to press to open it up. However, the container was sealed tight with no obvious way in. Letting out a sigh, he placed his hands on the front of the container and attempted to shake it. He looked around first to make sure no one could see him as he felt ridiculous for even trying it. The container didn't move and when Arnold kicked the door in frustration the metal container rang out with a tin like echo that filled the courtyard. None of his efforts worked and for a moment. He contemplated giving up and returning home.

Looking to the right he stared at the hieroglyph, the symbol it represented was an elk and that this was his grandad's spirit beast. Arnold knew that this was too much of a coincidence. He raised his hand to touch the hieroglyph and instantly felt his hand begin to tingle. He lowered it in shock and the sensation stopped immediately. Intrigued by the feeling, he raised his hand over the hieroglyph once more to find that his hand began to tingle again. The closer his hand got, the stronger the tingle became, to the point where it felt as though he had the worst pins and needles at the base of his palm. Feeling drawn to it, he pressed his hand against the symbol. The feeling in his hand became uncomfortable as he left his hand there for a moment, but nothing happened. Arnold recognised the pulsating sensation as similar to when his grandad transferred his auro to him before he passed.

"My auro," he said out loud. Closing his eyes, Arnold began to channel his auro. A soft blue glow began to emit around him. The tingling sensation in his hand began to subside and after a few moments, he heard a loud clunking noise as something moved behind the front panel of the storage crate. Further mechanical movement could be heard from the outside and the door became loose at the side. Arnold grabbed hold of the panel and began to slide it to the side, wanting to learn what awaited him on the inside. The light behind him illuminated the front part of the container, but beyond that, he could not see anything. Looking to the left of him he could see a switch. He walked across and pressed it, hoping it was for the lighting and to his great joy, it was. The fluorescent lights above him began to hum, followed by quick flickering before it became fully illuminated.

Arnold stood, momentarily confused by what he was looking at. All around him were his grandad's belongings, everything that was in his attic, everything that had been taken at the beginning of the week. Why would this all be here? This didn't make any sense. Who had done this? His thoughts were whirling around his head like a cyclone; this was bizarre. Why would someone take my grandad's stuff and bring it here in secret?

As he looked around, some of the items he recognised and others he didn't. The contents of the container looked as though they had been hastily added and there did not seem to be any order to how they were placed. Arnold instantly recognised the large chest where he had found the macuahuitl blade that was now at the Chichen. He recognised a couple of the glass cases with ornaments placed in them. There were other boxes scattered around the room too. Arnold continued to survey the space and noticed a small stool with an envelope placed on top with his name written on the front of it. Arnold felt a large lump in his throat as he recognised the handwriting immediately; it was his grandad's.

Pulling the paper out as fast as he could he began to read, his eyes stinging from the tears forming in his eyes.

Dear Arnold,

If you are reading this, then I am no longer here and you are at my storage container at Bramley lockup. You will have many questions and in time you will get answers. If you are wondering who has moved all of the contents of my attic here, then I will let you know that it is someone I used to work with at the Chichen and with whom I trust with my life.

As I explained to you, there are many an artefact in my possession that the Chichen do not know about and I fear what would happen if they were to fall into their hands. All these things laid out in front of you, they now all belong to you my boy and I could not think of a more deserving owner. You will find some old books and journals with age-old information around spirit beasts, shamans and many other mystical beasts as well as all these ancient relics and artefacts.

These mustn't fall into the wrong hands. If everything has gone to plan, then your father will believe they have been stolen and this must remain the case. He is too 'by the book' with regards to the Chichen and would allow them to be taken. I know you will look after them and keep them safe.

Finally, Arnold, I just wanted to let you know that I am so incredibly proud of you.

All my love

Grandad x

Arnold stared blankly at the letter, the stinging tears in his eyes beginning to stream down his face. He sobbed out loud and finally, Arnold was able to grieve for his grandad. He was able to say goodbye.

CHAPTER 5

Arnold woke the next morning feeling as though a huge weight had been lifted off him. Although he was confused by his grandad's belongings being moved to the Bramley lock up, the letter that was awaiting him there had helped him clear his head about his grandad's untimely death. He had messaged Everett when he had returned home to say he wanted to tell her something. She had replied saying she was in the middle of getting her things ready for school, so Arnold had told her he would catch up with her there. Today was their first day back at school following the end of the summer holidays. Quite a lot had happened in these holidays and Arnold was actually looking forward to being back in school. He felt a lot more confident in himself than he had in the previous year. After all, he was far more physically active, he had a spirit beast and he had a girlfriend.

As he sat at the breakfast table, a wave of sadness came over him as he realised that for the first time in a long time, Otto would not be knocking on for him so that they could walk to school together. Feeling deflated, Arnold stood up and pulled his bag out from underneath the stairs and placed it on his back. Opening the door, he exhaled with the realisation that he would not have his best friend to support him through their first year of being senior students. There wasn't much physical difference; his uniform hadn't changed apart from the tie that he was now wearing. The juniors at school wore a black and gold diagonal striped tie whereas now Arnold wore a completely black tie with the gold emblem of the school etched into the centre. Being a senior was more about the way it made Arnold feel. Walking the corridors of school felt different as no one tried to trip him up as he headed to his form room. Arnold suspected this was most likely down to his thicker set physique, making him more imposing.

Arnold took his seat in his form room, waiting for Mr. Tiggins to walk in to speak to them all and register them for the day. The girls were perched around a table on the far side of the room. They were talking about everything that had gone on in their lives over the summer. The boys were less reserved than this and were busy winding each other up about anything that came to mind, giggling and laughter filling the air. Arnold felt happy to be surrounded by such a positive atmosphere.

"Right guys, why is everyone not sat in their chairs?" Mr. Tiggins projected his voice into the classroom before he entered. Everyone looked like rabbits in the headlights and they quickly scattered to find their seats as fast as they could. Mr. Tiggins was Arnold's favorite teacher and he was pleased that he was going to be their form tutor this year. He naturally commanded respect from students with his perfectly balanced combination of wit and assertiveness. All the students knew they could have a laugh with him, but at the same time they knew where the line was and no one would cross it.

Mr. Tiggins walked in with his lunchbox under his arm. He was balancing a pile of papers in his hands, his sleeves rolled up on his green shirt and his tie not fully pulled to the top, making him look as though he had done a day's work before the school day had started. He swept his dark hair back to keep his fringe out of his eyes. He placed the papers on his desk before standing tall in front of everyone. Placing his hands in his pocket he started again, "That's more like it, guys. Good morning, everyone."

"Good morning, sir," the class repeated in unison.

"I hope you've all had a great summer. Ped - what have you been up to?"

"I spent the summer at the football academy." Andrew Pedder replied. His thick Scottish accent was as powerful and fierce as he was upfront.

"But Scotland can't play football," Mr. Tiggins laughed before he continued, "How was it?"

"Loved it! There were some scouts there from City," Andrew added excitedly. Andrew was a talent when it came to football and was already on the books at Blackburn Rovers, but he dreamt of playing for one of the top teams in the Premier League.

"Anyone else? What have you all been up to?" Mr. Tiggins asked while perched on his desk. Bethany Wright's hand shot up into the air such was her eagerness to speak.

"Sir, I went to Cuba with my family. It was amazing and I got to swim with dolphins." Her well-spoken voice did not echo the broad Lancashire accent that most other students had. Bethany was one of the more affluent kids in school and sometimes this could rub the other pupils up the wrong way.

"Wow, that sounds fantastic Betts," Mr. Tiggins responded, enthusiastically.

"Bethany sir, I don't like Betts," she quickly corrected.

Mr. Tiggins laughed before correcting himself. "Apologies, Bethany." He gave a sarcastic look to the rest of the class to acknowledge that he had been put in his place. "Now, Ethon - what have you been up to?" he asked. The room fell silent and Arnold felt tremendously awkward about it. He didn't want people feeling sorry for him because of his grandad, especially as no one knew what had really happened to him. All they did know is that he had died. Arnold stuttered with his words momentarily before answering.

"I...I... have just been training really, sir."

"Like Andrew at the Academy?" Mr. Tiggins replied.

"No, sir, at the Chichen." He answered quickly, not wanting to make a big deal of it. Before school had finished, people had been looking at him like he had three heads and Arnold did not want it to go back to that.

"Ah, I would ask what that entails, but I know you are not allowed to say." Sensing the awkward atmosphere in the room, Mr. Tiggins turned the conversation. "You can tell that you've been working hard lad. You look bigger. Are you trying to mimic The Rock or Jason Statham?" There was slight laughter in the room, creating a lighter atmosphere.

"More Cristian Bale in the Dark Knight Rises sir." Arnold laughed as he replied, which was echoed by further laughter around the classroom. Typically, he would have found himself blushing in this situation. On this occasion, he didn't.

There was a sudden knock at the door which caught the class off guard, the brisk rattle on the door making a couple of the students in the class jump. The door opened and Head of Year 10, Miss Elctree, walked in.

"Sorry to interrupt, we have a new pupil who has just moved to the area." She spoke straight to the point wishing not to be there any longer than she needed to be. "He is a bit nervous, but we have decided to place him in Form H as there is room here for a new addition. Please will you all welcome Marrok Lowe." Looking across at the door, she waved her hand for the newcomer to walk into the classroom. "Come on, boy." She ushered him into the room. Marrok walked into the classroom with both hands firmly fixed onto the shoulder straps of his backpack, a sure sign of nerves. His dark skin caught the sun as he entered the room, his number two haircut giving him a near shaven head look. He seemed pretty tall too, possibly a runner given his athletic frame. His piercing dark eyes surveyed the classroom he now found himself in and Arnold felt for him.

No one wanted to be the new kid at school as it could be hard to form friendships, especially when starting in the seniors. Miss Elctree left the room, leaving Marrok stood next to Mr. Tiggins.

"Welcome, Marrok." Mr. Tiggins placed a reassuring arm around the new boy and turned him to face the class. "You now need to sing a song to the class." Marrok looked panicked but was quickly reassured by Mr. Tiggins' laughter. "I'm just kidding lad! Can you just give everyone a quick introduction and then go sit over there by Ethon." Mr. Tiggins pointed across the room to draw Marrok's attention to the empty seat next to Arnold. The colour appeared to drain from him. Arnold again felt for him knowing that if it was him stood up there, his face would be bright red and he would be wishing for the ground to swallow him up.

"Hello, everyone, I'm Marrok." His voice was shaking slightly due to the pressure from everyone looking at him, his soft scouse accent faintly coming through. Arnold recognised the accent because he had members of his family from Liverpool, on his mum's side of the family. This was why he supported Everton. "I've just moved here from Cheshire with my mum and my sister." He looked around the room, not sure what else to say. "I like writing and football and I support Liverpool." There were a couple of cheers around the room from the boys who were also Liverpool supporters.

"Excellent," Mr. Tiggins interrupted. "Welcome to H form, please take a seat. Ethon, make sure you look after Marrok and help him settle in." Arnold was happy to help Marrok settle into school and liked the idea of having someone to sit next to in the form room for a change. Marrok walked over to the table, placing his bag underneath before sitting down next to Arnold. "Hi," he said, looking to start a conversation.

"Hey, just to warn you - I'm an Everton fan," Arnold quipped, trying to ease Marrok's nerves. Marrok shrugged.

"Well someone has to be." The two boys laughed as

they faced the front towards Mr. Tiggins who began to address the room again.

"Now need I remind everyone that you are now seniors within the school. I expect everyone that is associated with my form to set nothing but a positive example for others to follow." Removing his hands from his pockets, he picked up the pile of papers on his desk and began to walk around the room, distributing them to everyone. "Here are your timetables. Do NOT lose them. There are also application forms on my desk for anyone wishing to apply to be a prefect." As they were now seniors, they could be prefects which would look good on their CV when it came to looking at colleges and universities. Arnold didn't have any interest in being a prefect this year; he had enough to focus on with training at the Chichen. He knew he would also have to spend some time going through his Grandad's belongings at the lock-up and finding out who had attacked George earlier on that week. Arnold looked at his planner to see what the rest of the day held in store for him.

"Sweet, sports this afternoon," Marrok said out loud, clearly indicating what his favoured subject was.

"Me too," Arnold said. "The first class is always the worst though as they make us do all sorts of activities to test what level our fitness is at and who to pair us up with for the year."

Over the next hour the form went through the various classes, clubs and activities that were available this term. Marrok was quick to ask if there was a school paper he could join. The bell rang indicating that form was over and everyone could go for a break. The classroom emptied quickly and Arnold stood to put his items in his bag before swinging it around to put it on his shoulder.

"Mind if I stick with you during the break?" Marrok asked.

"Sure," Arnold responded. "I'm heading off to meet up with my friends Everett and George if you want to come?" Marrok nodded, appreciating Arnold's invitation and the two of them left the classroom and headed out to the central courtyard to meet the others. Navigating the corridors, they eventually made it back outside where there were students everywhere; every year group all in one place. Arnold couldn't help but think that from an aerial viewpoint, they must look like a colony of ants, with hundreds of kids doing different things in the courtyard. Some were chasing each other, some playing catch while others simply congregated or were playing football or basketball. A lot was going on and Arnold looked around the courtyard to find Everett and George. He was unable to make them out but once he used his enhanced vision, he was soon able to pick them out at the far end of the courtyard. "They're over there, this way," Arnold said, pointing and leading the way. Marrok stood squinting, unable to see how Arnold was able to make out where they were.

"How?" he began, "how can you see them from here?" Realising Marrok didn't know, Arnold began to explain while they walked across the courtyard.

"It's my spirit beast. It's an eagle, so one of the perks is I have perfect vision."

"That's pretty sweet," Marrok said, impressed with Arnold's spirit beast.

"How about you, do you have any special traits?" Arnold asked, knowing that it was rude to ask someone what their spirit beast was.

"Let's just say I have good senses," Marrok said, choosing not to let his spirit beast be known at this point.

"Hey." Everett smiled as the two of them reached the far side of the courtyard, looking bemused by the new face that accompanied Arnold. Her ice-blue eyes scanned over Marrok as she appeared to be weighing him up. Her hair was tied back into braids, which was her preferred hairstyle.

"Hi." George smiled at Marrok, taken aback by his good looks. She had her beany on with a few red curls poking out at the front. Her uniform was pristine as ever as she took great pride in her appearance at school. Both stood there for a moment, eyes fixed on Marrok and no more words were spoken for a few moments. Sensing the awkwardness from the lack of an introduction, Arnold stepped in.

"This is Marrok. He's new and in my form. He's just moved here. Marrok, this is Everett and George." He placed his hand out to highlight who was who.

"Hi," Marrok responded, sheepishly.

"What brings you to Oswald?" George enquired, unable to take her eyes off him. "Bit of a random place to move to."

"That's what I thought. If I'm honest, I had never heard of Oswald before my mum mentioned she had an interview for a job here." Marrok seemed to be relaxing into the conversation now.

"And what does she do?" George pried further. Her interrogation techniques definitely needed working on.

"She's a reporter," Marrok replied. "She's just got a job as an editor at the Oswald advertiser."

"What?"

"George!" Everett interjected at George's persistent questions. "Sorry Marrok, she isn't very good at talking to new boys." George looked far from happy with Everett for stopping her asking questions and at her comments about her not being good around boys. "What session have you guys got next? We have sports," Everett said, pulling a face. "No doubt Mr. Phillips will be drilling us all as per usual at the start of the year." Arnold tried to change the direction of the conversation, shifting the attention away from Marrok to allow him some freedom from the constant questioning.

"Us too," he said. The bell began to ring, meaning that it was time for sports, the first bell indicating that they had five minutes to get to the changing rooms.

"I'll catch up with you at lunch and fill you in on last night," Arnold called to the girls as they walked away.

"No worries. See you then," Everett replied.

Arnold didn't want to give too much away, having only

just met Marrok. He didn't know him well enough to talk about the storage container and his Grandad's belongings. They made their way back across the courtyard and over to the sports block.

As Arnold stood with Marrok outside the changing rooms waiting for Mr. Phillips, Otto walked in through the doorway and walked straight past them towards the back of the line that had formed. Arnold looked at Otto intently hoping that he would at the very least acknowledge him, but he didn't. Instead, Otto stood at the back of the line focusing on the door into the changing room. He looked utterly disinterested in being there, as though he could not wait to get away. Arnold contemplated going over to speak to him but he did not want to face the embarrassment in front of everyone if he was to be ignored again.

"Everything ok with you two?" Marrok asked, sensing the tension coming from Arnold.

"We used to be best friends but now he won't even acknowledge me," Arnold sighed.

The shrill sound of a whistle could be heard and Mr. Phillips walked past in his usual tracksuit bottoms and sweatshirt and unlocked the changing room door. Mr. Phillips was - at a guess - in his mid-thirties and his hair had started to grey around his sideburns but as a PE teacher, he was in peak physical fitness. "Right boys, get dressed and line up in the sports hall. We are going to start with a bleep test." A considerable groan erupted from the line of boys, the bleep test was their least favourite test and Arnold just wanted to get it over with.

Around fifteen minutes later, the boys and girls of year ten stood lined up across the bottom of the sports hall. Some were excited by the prospect of being physically pushed, some were dreading it and some were not even entertaining the idea of completing the bleep test. Mr. Phillips stood in front of them, alongside Mrs. Bramble. She was the girls' sports teacher, her personality as spikey as her name implied.

"Most of you have done this before but for those that haven't, Mrs. Bramble will explain what the bleep test entails." Mr. Phillips blew his whistle sharply to gather the attention of the few students that were talking to each other and not paying attention. Mrs. Bramble stepped forward to address the sports hall. "You will all start on the line in the centre of the sports hall. Once you hear the bleep, you will set off running to the far side of the hall before the next bleep sounds. If you have not made it before the bleep then you are out. You will continue with this for as long as you can with the beeps getting closer together until neither a boy nor girl remains. This is a test of endurance, don't overdo it early on and good luck."

"Boys you are on the left-hand side of the hall with me and girls you are on the right with Mrs. Bramble." Mr. Phillips directed and blew his whistle once more, pushing everyone to line up where he had indicated. There was nervous talk in the room as everyone hurriedly tried to get to the right part of the sports hall before the bleep test would begin. Arnold lined up with the crowd of other boys on the right side of the hall as directed. He felt confident that he would do ok at this today given the amount of training that he had been doing recently. Last year had been an embarrassment with him falling over just a few rounds in. Otto and Andrew Pedder were the last ones standing, with Andrew eventually winning. Arnold exhaled as he tried to focus. As long as he didn't repeat last year's disaster, he was happy with however long he lasted. The first bleep sounded and everyone set of running apart from a few at the back who had decided their plan was to walk and be eliminated at the sound of the first bleep. Arnold began at a steady pace and simply focused on the line at the edge of the hall, making it with plenty of time to spare before the next bleep. Those that did not make it in time were directed to stand at the side of the hall and the rest simply turned and began to run back towards the opposite line before the next bleep sounded.

Arnold continued his steady pace for around five minutes as the number of people taking part got fewer and fewer. He had already made it past the stage that he managed last time, so Arnold was happy, but he felt like he still had quite a bit left in the tank. Mr. Phillips continued to push those remaining and announcing how many were remaining.

"Last ten, keep going!" Mr. Phillips encouraged as the next bleep sounded. The pace was picking up now and Arnold began to notice the metallic taste in his mouth from his exertion. Making it to the other side before the bleep, he started running back towards the other side along with the last six boys. As he reached the far side, the bleep sounded again.

"Four left! Keep going - you are all doing brilliantly!" Mr. Phillips exclaimed. Arnold couldn't believe that he had made it to this point; he had far exceeded what he had expected. He was surprised by how much his fitness had improved over the summer. Arnold glanced across to see who the other remaining runners were. Marrok, Otto and Andrew were still in the test with him as he continued running, only just meeting the bleep this time and knowing that he was nearly done. Digging in, Arnold gritted his teeth and sprinted back as fast as he could hoping to make the next bleep. Reaching the line but unsure if he had made it, he turned to go again but was stopped by Mr. Phillips. "Ethon, Pedder you're out, well done."

Happy with what he had achieved, Arnold moved to the side of the hall while breathing heavily, trying to regain his breath. He picked up his bottle of water and began to gulp it down, hoping to get some refreshment from it. He looked over at the other side to see all the girls had finished. It looked as though Everett and George had done well as they were hugging each other and looked as though they were also still trying to catch their breath.

Arnold's attention drifted back to the boy's side as Otto and Marrok were still going for it. The hall began to erupt with cheers and shouting as everyone tried to encourage them both to keep going. Both looked determined, but Otto looked more focused like he had nothing else in his mind but to reach the other side before the next bleep. Both were at the point where they were sprinting each time to make it across.

"Come on guys, you've got this," Arnold shouted, wanting both to win. The two of them continued, only just making the bleep but getting faster and faster each time. Arnold was amazed at the speed and the endurance they were exhibiting. They turned after the next bleep and sprinted as fast as they could to the other side. They appeared to be neck and neck until Marrok began to pull away slightly, just making the bleep before Otto could reach the line.

"Redburn, you're done. Fantastic effort!" Mr. Phillips clapped, as Marrok continued his run.

Marrok put his head down and pushed himself to make it across the line one last time. again just meeting the beep. He was exhausted, but he had won.

Loud cheer erupted from all around the hall at Marrok's achievement. He had won the bleep test and by the look of it, he had beaten the school record by some way.

The shrill whistle blew once more. "Fantastic Lowe, absolutely fantastic." Mr. Phillips walked across to him, the noise of his clap drowning out the pupils that were talking to each other. Arnold looked over to see where Otto was; he had moved to the corner of the room and was taking a drink.

"Right, everyone. Take a break for fifteen minutes and then come back here. Next up is the accuracy test," Mrs. Bramble announced. Another test that Arnold had failed miserably last year - Archery. Last time, Arnold couldn't even use a bow and didn't make it through the first round. This time though Arnold had been receiving weapon training at the Chichen and although he had not done much training with one, he knew he could now at least fire an arrow.

He walked across to Marrok to congratulate him on the bleep test. Everett and George had already beaten him in getting to him and he arrived as they both finished giving him a hug.

"You were amazing!" George gasped as she pulled away from hugging him.

"You are so fast!" Arnold said. He and Otto had been training at the Chichen and had increased abilities because of their connections through the Ch'ahb' and he had still beaten them.

"I told you," Marrok panted as his breath began to regulate. "I'm into my sports." He smiled at the others, clearly grateful for their support.

"You did amazing, too!" Everett announced as she gave Arnold a hug.

"After your trip last year, I'm surprised you turned up," George teased. Arnold laughed, not taking her comments to heart.

Before long, the whistle blew again and it was time to line up for the archery test. Everyone was split into five groups with targets lined up a quarter of the way up the sports hall.

"Right guys you all know the drill. You hit anywhere within the target you go through. You miss, you are out. It's that simple," Mr. Phillips explained.

"Don't forget that after two rounds, the targets will then be moved further back until we are down to the final person," Mrs. Bramble finished.

The first row of people lined up to take their shot with the bow and arrow. Everett was up first out of their group and hit the target meaning she was through to the next round. Unfortunately, George didn't, meaning that she was eliminated in the first round; Otto and Marrok hit the target with ease. Arnold stepped forward and picked the bow up from the previous student and reached into the quiver next to him to retrieve an arrow. He focused on the centre of the target and took a slow deep breath. Pulling the arrow back against the bowstring, he let go. The arrow fired into the centre of the target. Arnold surprised himself with his accuracy and simply shrugged it off as beginner's luck. Walking back, he passed the bow to Everett and smiled, feeling slightly smug at his achievement. After another round, the targets were moved back to the halfway point. This time Marrok missed, meaning that he was out with Arnold, Everett and Otto all hitting the target. Again, after another round, the targets were moved back into the final quarter of the sports hall. Everett and Otto had hit the target in the first round with Everett only just managing it. Bethany Wright had missed meaning she was out. Only the three of them remained, that was if Arnold hit the target.

Arnold took hold of the bow and felt his nerves increase, very much aware that everyone in the hall had eyes on him. Arnold used his enhanced vision to focus directly on the centre of the target. Understanding the trajectory courtesy of those that had gone before him, he raised his bow slightly, before pulling the arrow back and letting go. Arnold exhaled as the arrow fired across the sports hall and pierced the target, hitting the yellow zone just off the centre of the target. He was more than happy with that. He turned and smiled at Everett as he gave her the bow for her second turn. This time Everett narrowly missed the target meaning that she was eliminated and it was down to Otto and Arnold. They both followed up by hitting the target once more.

The targets were now moved to the far side of the sports hall and could not go any further.

"Just to make you aware, no one has ever hit the target from this range," Mr. Phillips informed everyone. Two targets sat at the bottom of the other end of the hall. Both boys with a bow and arrow in hand. Otto stepped forward first, pulled his arrow back and fired it quickly and without hesitation. He hit the target and the students began to clap and cheer. Feeling under pressure, Arnold stepped forward for his turn and again used his enhanced vision to focus on his target. He raised his bow higher up in the air and inhaled slowly before firing the arrow across the room. A second after he fired it, he heard the noise of it hitting the target. Everyone began cheering for him hitting the target too. Otto stepped forward while the students were still cheering and fired his second arrow, which was in the red circle within the centre of the target. He was completely calm and composed, only focused on one thing; beating Arnold. Feeling taken aback by how quickly and easily Otto had taken his shot and hit the target, Arnold stepped forward. He removed an arrow to take his shot.

"Ethon, if you hit this whoever is closest to the centre will take first place. Miss and Redburn takes it," Mr. Phillips said, continuing with his commentary from the sidelines. Arnold took aim, focusing on the centre of his target. He then glanced across at Otto's target. Seeing that his shot was just off centre, Arnold knew he would have to pretty much hit a perfect shot to win. Arnold tried to focus on his target but found himself distracted by once again looking at Otto's target. Taking a deep breath, he drew his arrow back, seemingly focusing on both targets simultaneously. Arnold could feel a tingling sensation in his hand, the same sensation he felt when he was summoning his spirit beast. He raised his bow once more and fired the arrow. As it set off, he noticed that he had seemingly fired two arrows. One l normal but the other was glowing a bright blue colour. One arrow flew into his target but the glowing arrow hit Otto's target at the same time as his own. He had hit both targets and upon closer inspection (courtesy of his enhanced vision) both were pretty much in the centre of the targets.

The sports hall didn't erupt with cheers; everyone just stood staring in awe at what Arnold had just done. An eery quietness interrupted only by the whispers from his classmates.

"He's spirit wielded a weapon!" Marrok whispered to Everett and George. "That just doesn't happen."

"Spirit what?" Everett asked, not understanding this term.

"He's connected to the spirit world to wield a spirit weapon," he continued.

"Ethon, what the hell was that?" Mr. Phillips roared across the hall. Arnold shrugged, confused.

"I don't know, sir," Arnold replied, obviously shaken by what had just occurred. Mr. Phillips paused for a moment before beginning to slowly clap.

"That was amazing! We have our winner!" he shouted. The hall began clapping and cheering at Arnold's victory. This was something he had never experienced before for two reasons; not only were people cheering for him, but he had also just discovered a new ability that he had no idea he was capable of.

CHAPTER 6

"How the hell did you do that?" George was stunned and unable to process what she had just witnessed Arnold do. "You fired a light bow out of your hand. How?" she demanded. The four of them sat in the school hall, eating their lunches.

Everyone was buzzing about what had just happened in the sports hall. Arnold firing an arrow made of light had spread around the school faster than the recent fires on Rivington moors due to the heatwave.

Arnold looked sheepishly around the room as he noticed that the vast majority of people within the hall sat whispering to each other. They were intermittently looking in Arnold's direction, making him feel paranoid. He had lasted one morning without everyone looking at him like he was different and now it was back to how it was last year.

"What did you call it?" Everett asked Marrok. "When it happened, you seemed to know what to call it."

"It's called spirit wielding. I didn't know it was an actual thing though," Marrok answered. "My mum used to tell me stories about it. It's where you use your auro to draw energy from the spirit world to form a weapon. I'm sure my mum said you needed an artefact to help draw the energy but

Arnold seemed to do it without using one."

"I haven't got a clue how I did it," Arnold said, not understanding what had happened. He wanted to be at the Chichen so he could ask his dad about spirit wielding. "I will talk to my dad when I get to the Chichen. He will know about it." Wishing it was the end of the day, Arnold wanted to get the final part of the fitness test completed so that he could finish and head off. He had so much to do between the lock-up, finding out what had attacked George and how he had spirit wielded.

"And Marrok you were so fast in the bleep test," George said, gazing at Marrok with adoring eyes, clearly smitten with the new boy.

"Football, rugby and track sports," he replied. "It's all I've ever done since I was little."

"Still, you beat Arnold and Otto who have had specialist training," Everett added.

"It's nothing special." Marrok was trying to play down his achievement. However, the look on Everett and George's faces implied that he had not been successful. "You were talking before about the Chichen?" Marrok turned the conversation back to Arnold.

"Arnold and Otto were allowed to join the Chichen," George answered quickly and without hesitation.

"We declined," Everett added.

"What, how is that?" Marrok looked interested in what he had just been told.

"It's a long story," Arnold said, feeling there were more pressing topics to discuss.

"That's awesome, you shouldn't have been allowed to join until you were eighteen," Marrok continued.

"We know." Arnold, Everett and George replied in unison.

The four of them continued to eat their lunch and regain some energy after the morning's activities. Talking about how Arnold had spirit wielded an arrow and what this meant.

"I need to tell you about the lock-up, too." Arnold needed to explain and had decided that Marrok was trustworthy enough to share this information with. "I managed to get into it last night." Marrok stood there with a puzzled expression on his face, not understanding what Arnold was referring to.

"And? What's in it?" Everett pressed, wanting to know the contents straight away. Arnold looked around him to ensure no one else was listening in and leant forward to speak quietly to the others.

"My granddad's stuff," his words almost a whisper. "It went missing from his house and has been moved there."

"That doesn't make any sense. Why would someone do that?" Everett responded, leaning in towards the huddle that they had formed.

"I don't know, but whoever has done it doesn't want the Chichen to know. I think there are artefacts there," Arnold added.

"What?" George spoke loudly, drawing attention to them and Everett quickly elbowed her to tell her to keep quiet. "Arnold if there are artefacts, you need to hand them over to the Chichen."

"Ever the responsible one," Everett teased. Arnold smiled.

"The note said not to and until I know why, they will stay in the lock-up. If we meet up after school, I will show you everything."

The school bell began to ring, meaning that they all needed to head back to the sports hall to finish the final part of the PE test. The last session of the day was a strength endurance test and Arnold felt confident he would be ok this time around. They headed back across the courtyard and made their way into the sports hall alongside the rest of the students taking part. Standing along a line across the side of the sports hall, they all waited patiently for direction from Mr. Phillips and Mrs. Bramble.

"Pair up everyone," Mr. Phillips instructed. "You all

know the drill. I want to see how many press-ups you can do in five minutes, the same for sit-ups. Then I want to see how many pull-ups you can do. Alternate between each of them while the other person counts how many you have done." He blew his whistle to indicate that the final test had now started.

Arnold looked at Marrok intending to pair up with him however, George had beaten him to it and quickly hopped in front of him like a giddy child.

"You're with me," she announced, her tone not really giving Marrok any choice at all. Arnold laughed and walked over to Everett to pair up, but she put her hand up to him to stop him in his tracks.

"Er, no, I am not your back up. I saw you walking to Marrok." Everett walked over to Lizzy Hargreave and spoke with her, making it clear to Arnold that she had paired up with someone else.

Arnold looked around the hall awkwardly realising that everyone had been paired up. Marrok had already begun his sit-ups. George sat at his feet, gazing at him adoringly most likely forgetting to count.

"Ethon, what are you doing?" Mr. Phillips bellowed from the other side of the hall, his voice reverberating around the walls. "Redburn, Ethon - pair up now!" Arnold could see that Otto had set up by himself and had already dropped to the floor and started with his press-ups. "Those don't count Redburn! Pair up – Arnold, start counting." Mr. Phillips wasn't giving the two the option to decline. Feeling awkward, he walked across the room to Otto and began to count his press-ups out loud. Otto didn't look up or even acknowledge Arnold being there, simply carrying on his press-ups at a steady pace. Arnold continued to count and looked at Otto in amazement as his speed did not falter. He continued with his press-ups for the remainder of the five minutes without stopping, when most others in the room were busy collapsing or stopping for breaks.

Mr. Phillips blew his whistle and they swapped over.

Arnold got into the press-up position and he looked up towards Otto, who was looking directly at him. He felt as though he was looking straight through him. His green eyes looking vacant as though Otto's mind was somewhere else. Arnold contemplated asking him what was on his mind. Still, he opted against doing this as he knew he would most likely ignore him again. Lowering himself to the floor, he pushed himself back up and heard Otto start to count. He still has a voice then, Arnold thought to himself, becoming more frustrated at Otto's persistent coldness towards him. Arnold managed to keep up a steady pace during the press-ups exercise but nowhere near the speed that Otto had managed to maintain. The whistle sounded, the two switched around again and Otto got into the sit-up position. Arnold sat at his feet to hold them down. Otto began with his sit-ups, again at a fast pace. He looked focused and continued to look only forward as he inhaled and exhaled, quickly and steadily. When it came to Arnold, he had done better than last year, but he knew that he had managed nothing as close to as many as Otto had. The whistle blew for the final time and Arnold stopped and sat up to catch his breath; this would have killed him in previous years. Thankfully, due to his training at the Chichen, he had found it relatively easy this time around.

The whole hall erupted into a series of moans and groans and students lay sprawled out across the hall, exhausted from their combined ten minutes of exercise. Everett was sat up catching her breath and Marrok stood over George, laughing as he extended his hand to help her up from the ground which she playfully accepted. Her face was bright red from either the exercise or blushing.

"Lowe, Redburn, by the bars, please." Mrs. Bramble barked her orders as she scribbled notes on her clipboard before sliding her pen into her hair. The two of them walked over to the pull-up bars and awaited further instruction. "Clearly, you two are miles ahead of everyone else in this class." Her voice stern, she was very matter of fact in her approach. "I want you to take hold of the bars and begin to do pull-ups, you will do a pull up on my count. The last one to be on the bars will win." The sports hall became restless with the excitement of the other students as everyone began to form a large half-circle around the two of them as they jumped and took hold of the bars. The two of them looked physically well-matched despite Otto having a slightly more substantial frame.

"Up," Mrs. Bramble directed. The two of them completed their first pull up as directed. Mrs. Bramble repeated this process every few seconds, with the two of them successfully completing a pull-up. The hall began to come to life as the students began to shout the name of who they wanted to win. Arnold felt conflicted but decided to call out the name of who he wanted to win.

"Come on Marrok, you've got this." Looking at the pair of them, he noticed straight away that Otto's fixed gaze changed as he stared across at Arnold. He looked even more determined as he picked up his pace on the bars. Marrok saw what Otto was doing and also upped his pace, attempting to keep up with Otto. Everyone continued to cheer and roar the two of them on, with Mrs. Bramble giving up on trying to direct the pace. Sweat was pouring off both of them. It seemed neither of them planned to let the other win. Marrok began to slow first and was clearly now struggling, his hands slowly slipping before he lost his grip altogether and dropped to the ground below. He crouched down and then stood up to stretch while panting heavily to gather his breath. Otto continued to look forward and continued to complete his pull-ups at the same pace.

The hall began to cheer for Otto, who had won the final test. Arnold was amazed at his physical capabilities and he was pretty sure that he had just broken every school record going.

"That's enough, Redburn." Mr. Phillips raised his whistle for the final time to close the proceedings. Otto dropped from the bars and headed to the exit, ignoring everyone that had walked over to congratulate him as if they were not there.

"That was impressive." George stood next to Marrok in admiration. "He's had training. You did awesomely." Her cheesy smile to Marrok showing that she clearly fancied him.

"Why's Otto being so weird?" Everett spoke as she drew level with Arnold and the others.

"I'm sure he will tell us when he's ready." Arnold hoped that this would be the outcome but at the moment it felt as though he had completely lost his best friend. He did have the slightest glimmer of hope given that he seemed to react when he had cheered on Marrok. "I need to get to the Chichen to see Dad and ask him about spirit wielding. Meet me at the lock-up at six." Everett, George and Marrok agreed and Arnold left the sports hall, grabbing his bag before heading to the Chichen. He headed out of the school gates, walking at a pace to get there as quickly as he could.

Arriving at the Chichen, he ran up the steep stone steps and made his way through the large, intricately detailed, circular wooden door at the entrance.

"Is my dad around?" he asked Grace tentatively as he entered. Grace looked up from her computer, pushing her large framed spectacles up her nose so she could get a better look at Arnold.

"Arthur is upstairs in his office."

"Thanks." Arnold walked past the reception area and made his way towards his dad's office, so desperate to speak to him that he forgot to knock, walking straight in. Arthur was sat at his dark wood desk, a fan sat at the side of him pointing in his direction to cool him down due to the excessive heat they were currently experiencing. He looked irritable as he quickly grabbed some papers that were just about to take flight courtesy of the fan.

"You might be my son, Arnold, but you need to knock before you come in. We are not at home," he said sternly, taking his irritability out on Arnold.

"Sorry dad," Arnold said sheepishly. "Something happened at school today, something I need you to explain to me."

Looking up from his paperwork, his dad removed his reading glasses from his face and placed them on the desk next to his pile of papers. "Go on?"

Arnold hastily began. "We were doing Archery today and I fired an arrow that wasn't there. It was the same colour as my auro, it felt like when I summon my spirit beast but different. Like it was in my hands." His speech was fast as he was trying to offload all this information to his dad so he could get the answers he wanted just as quickly.

"What?" Arthur looked surprised. "Are you sure? Did anyone see?"

"The whole sports hall," said Arnold.

"You spirit wielded? How?" Arthur pressed him for more answers.

"I don't know, dad." Arnold replied, "That's why I am asking you."

"But you haven't got an artefact?" His dad's face looked more perplexed. "You wielded pure energy from the spirit world using just your raw auro?" Unsure if he was speaking to him directly or just thinking out loud, Arnold walked towards the desk and sat down opposite his dad while he gathered his thoughts.

"What are you on about, dad?" Arthur appeared to realise he was talking out loud and brought himself back to the conversation, brushing his hands down his thick moustache before looking at Arnold and continuing.

"It's unheard of for someone your age to spirit wield. Only the most skilled Elders can manipulate energy. Even then, they need to use an artefact to harness the power. Like the hilt of a blade or the shaft from a spear. The relics are artefaced by a Shaman which means with the right knowledge, experience and skill an Elder can produce the blade of that weapon from pure energy directly from the spirit world. These weapons are incredibly powerful and extremely dangerous." Arthur's voice had a serious tone as he explained in detail to Arnold. "The Chichen are responsible for storing these artefacts to make sure they don't fall into the wrong hands. Clearly, the bow at school will not be an artefact which means you have naturally wielded pure energy in your hands without one. Naturally, we will have to acquire those bows from school to carry out the necessary tests." He looked at Arnold with concern. "We need to manage this. You said everyone in the hall saw you do this?" Arnold nodded as he tried to absorb everything his dad had said. "Everyone will be sharing that you have done this. You need to be careful because this is going to draw even more attention to you. I need to speak with Mr. Whitaker so he can advise us on what to do. Go and do some training and I will catch up with you later."

Arnold stood up from the desk and left, making his way to the training room where he spent the next hour alone. He trained intently with his grandad's Machuahuitl, which he had been using all summer and now kept at the Chichen. He was only just starting to get used to the weight of it and knew he was a lot more effective with it than he had been when he needed to defend himself against Levent at the tower.

When he had finished practicing with the weapon, he placed it in the weapons rack, before walking over to his bag and removing a towel to wipe the sweat from his face. He walked back down the corridor towards the changing rooms, grabbing a quick shower before getting changed into the spare clothes that he left at the Chichen. He didn't want to put his school uniform back on when he was going to head straight to the lock-up to see the others. Dressed in his dark grey jogging bottoms and his Everton shirt, he placed his trainers on and headed out of the changing rooms. As he exited, he saw Mr. Whitaker and Mr. Redburn walking into Mr. Whitaker's office. Mr. Redburn saw Arnold and shot him a look of utter disgust. Arnold felt confused as he had no idea why Otto's dad now hated him so much. He also wondered why he would be having a meeting at the Chichen when he was now so seemingly against them. Not knowing whether his dad would have spoken to anyone yet. Arnold decided he would catch up with him at home later and headed off to the lock-up.

CHAPTER 7

Arnold arrived late at the lockup to find George, Everett and Marrok waiting for him.

"Did you see your Dad?" Everett asked, leaning against the storage container with her arms folded.

"Yeah, he hasn't really gone into that much detail. Just said that normally only elders can spirit wield. I'm waiting to see what Mr. Whitaker advises." Arnold walked up to the front of the container and held his hand over the elk hieroglyph. His hand began to tingle again. The mechanism behind could be heard unlocking and Arnold pulled the door back to reveal the contents to the others.

"Wow!" Marrok took his hands out of his pocket while admiring the items that were stored inside.

"This is pretty cool," Everett said, stepping inside the container to take a closer look.

"Pretty strange more like." George didn't look impressed. "It's too easy. Why would someone move all this stuff here?" Everett cast her a skeptical look before she continued looking around at everything.

"What is all this stuff?"

"Stuff my grandad accumulated over the years from different countries. Do you think there are any artefacts in here?" He picked up a misshapen bowl and blew the dust off it to inspect it closer before placing it back on the side.

"What the hell is that?" Marrok asked, pointing at one of the glass cabinets. Arnold looked across but did not recognise the thing that Marrok was pointing at. On a little table stood an ancient, worn, stone figurine. The large head of the figurine had squinted eyes and a mouth that implied it was meant to denote either anger or sadness. Down the sides of each side of its head, there were symmetrical raised parts that looked like pointed ears. "I've never seen this before; it looks like it's wearing a hat." The small statue's arms sat in front of it with its hands connecting to each other. The carvings on it were not clear due to it being worn away.

"It's a headdress," George explained. "It looks really old, Arnold. Headdresses usually mean it's of high ranking from wherever it's from."

"It's giving me the creeps." Everett was not impressed with the small statue and made it clear that she did not like it. "Can we turn it around so it's not looking at us? I feel like it's watching us." Marrok walked over to the peculiar item laughing and turned the old, worn statue around, so it was facing the opposite way.

"Better. Thank you." Everett smiled at Marrok and began rummaging through some of the boxes.

George was also searching through some boxes at the back. She covered her mouth, trying her hardest not to breathe in any of the dust that rose into the air as she opened each new box. "Books…these look really old too, guys. I really think we should be handing this stuff over to the Chichen."

"No!" Arnold snapped. "My grandad kept this stuff away from the Chichen for a reason, we need to find out why."

"Sounds good to me," Marrok agreed.

"Me too," added Everett.

"If you insist, but it doesn't mean I am happy," George said, frowning.

Over the next hour, the four of them continued to

search through everything within the garage. They found mainly ornamental items such as the strange statue, various bowls and vases and a couple of large cups that were more akin to chalices. Marrok's phone went off, indicating he had a text. Looking at it, he sighed. "I need to head off, guys. My mum wants me home." They all said their goodbyes, then Marrok left the container and made his way down the overgrown path until he could no longer be seen.

Arnold was opening the only box that remained unexamined in the corner of the container. He unfolded the interlocking cardboard to reveal that the box was full of more books, even older than the ones George had found. On the top of the pile lay a strange leather-bound book with no title etched into it. The outside of the book had a border that was imprinted into the leather. Within the centre of the book sat a turquoise stone, fixed into the cover with a pattern indented into the leather around it. Arnold took hold of the book and removed it from the box. He felt drawn to the book; it had a strange feel to it and Arnold could feel his hands throbbing slightly. It was a similar sensation to how it felt when placing his hand on the hieroglyph to unlock the storage container. Intrigued by the design, he took a large gulp of breath and then blew on the book. A thick layer of dust formed a small cloud which headed towards George as she was rummaging through a drawer next to him. She began coughing as the dust engulfed her, firing a disapproving look at Arnold in the process. "What's that?" she spluttered.

His gaze fixed on the stone on the cover, he opened the book. Flicking through the pages, he could see various handwritten entries. They looked old if the outdated handwriting style was anything to go by and there were detailed sketches and drawings of differing spirit beasts, emblems, totems and hieroglyphs. "It looks like a journal," Arnold said.

"Any name on it?" Everett asked.

Flicking the book from the back to the front, he looked

to see if he could make out a name anywhere. Something seemed familiar to Arnold, as he looked intently at the scribed words within the journal. A spark ignited in his head and he walked over to one of the cabinets, opened a drawer and removed an envelope. It was the letter from his grandad that was in the lockup when he first managed to get inside. Pulling out the letter, he unfolded it and placed it next to the journal, matching the handwriting. "It's my grandad's," he confirmed, before putting his letter back down on the side. Arnold wondered if this was why he was drawn to it and loved that he had something that his grandad had written when he was younger. He wanted to go home now to read it all.

Arnold was so distracted by the book that he did not notice the low grumbling noise coming from outside of the storage container.

"What's that noise?" Everett asked, the noise growing louder as it approached. George froze. She knew exactly what it was.

"Oh no. It's back."

Everett ran to the entrance of the container and pulled the door shut quickly locking the three of them inside. There was a loud roar followed by a bang, as the spirit beast threw itself at the door, the noise echoing around the container. It was quiet for a few moments and then there was another loud bang; the beast was trying to get inside.

"What are we going to do?" George's voice trembled as she spoke.

"We wait it out," Everett said with a degree of confidence. "We need to ring for help."

"We can't. If we do, they will find this place and that's not what my grandad wanted," Arnold said, a pleading tone to his voice. Looking around the room to plan the next move, Arnold couldn't see anything he could use as a weapon. There was an old coat stand in the corner and instinctively he walked over to it and snapped the end off, creating a make-shift spear. "We are going to open that door. As soon as I get out there, you shut the door behind me. Ok?" He stood behind the door and nodded for Everett to pull it open. Wouldn't Everett argue?

Arnold stepped out from the container and braced himself for what was coming. The container shut behind him and he knew he was on his own now, but there was no spirit beast to be seen. Arnold brought his make-shift spear into the air and held it in a defensive position. He began walking through the overgrown grass within the walls of the storage unit. Walking slowly, he could feel his adrenaline had spiked and his senses felt supercharged. He continued to walk around the grounds, knowing that whatever this spirit beast was it was in here with him. The sun was on its decline due to it being late evening and it was casting dramatic shadows around the grounds, creating an eerie environment. Arnold could hear some rustling and turned to see what it was. He was too slow, the spirit beast was on him within a moment, sending him crashing into the side of the storage container behind him. Picking himself up from the floor, Arnold reached to pick up the spear that lay on the floor beside him.

Stood in front of him was the spirit beast that had attacked George. He recognised the green, glowing eyes and auro surrounding it. The beast stood on two legs, its enormous frame slightly yellow in colour with black circular markings dotted around its skin. Its large teeth protruded out of its mouth as it stood growling at Arnold, its large claws visible from its opened hands. This didn't fit the profile of any spirit beast he had ever learnt about before. It was not clear to him what animal this beast was but the way it stood suggested it was more human than animal.

The beast ran at him once more and stretched its clawed hand out to swipe at Arnold who managed to dive to the side. The creature missed and clawed down the side of the container, drawing sparks from the impact. Arnold spun around and swung his spear, hitting the creature on the back with it with as much force as he could muster. The impact snapped the frail weapon as soon as it connected with its muscular back. Swiping its arm out again, Arnold jumped back to avoid it, but the large claws caught his arm, slicing his flesh. He winced and placed his hand over his arm; he needed a weapon against this spirit beast as its claws were proving problematic.

Arnold picked up the broken spear once more just so he had something to defend himself with and began to motion his bloodied arm in the air to summon his eagle. The soft blue glow from his auro began to emit and within a moment, his spirit beast had appeared to assist him. Sensing that he had an injury, the eagle stood in front of Arnold and fully extended its impressive wingspan, shielding him from the beast that had attacked him. Moving forward at speed, the eagle took flight at the strange beast that stood in front of it and sank its talons into the beast's shoulders, lifting it off into the air. Using its momentum, the eagle suddenly let go, sending the spirit beast crashing into the side of a storage container. The force created a significant dent in the side of the metal casing. The beast climbed up from the floor and ran at Arnold once more. In an all-out frenzy, it began to slice and swipe at the eagle. The eagle had no option but to use its enormous wings to bat its claws away, before landing on top of a storage container out of its reach. The beast climbed up after the eagle with minimal effort and continued its volley of attacks. The eagle flew towards it once more and attempted to grab the beast with its talons as before, but this time the beast was wise to the plan of attack. It grabbed hold of the eagle's feet and began spinning it through the air as if competing in a hammer throw event in the Olympics. After turning a few times, it let go, launching the eagle through the air and it bounced off the uneven ground before them before eventually sliding to a stop in front of Arnold. Arnold dropped to his knees as he felt the pain through his connection to his spirit beast and his back and sides began to throb.

Arnold looked at his hands and feeling the strange

tingling sensation within them, they began to glow through his auro. Hoping for the best, he began to focus on the raw energy he could draw on from the spirit world as he attempted to spirit wield once more. His knees trembled as he tried to get to his feet. Nothing was happening, he was unable to spirit wield when he needed to the most.

The feral beast dropped down from the container it was stood on and ran at Arnold once more with relentless speed. It threw itself through the air, landing a dropkick in the centre of his chest sending Arnold tumbling backwards once more. Arnold's arms were weak, he was gasping for breath as he attempted to get up. He collapsed back on the floor, unable to pick himself up again. He could hear the feral snarling of the spirit beast as it walked over to him. Its strange markings caught Arnold's attention and he stared at the razor-sharp teeth on show. Arnold felt himself being scooped into the air as if he weighed nothing and the beast pulled him towards its face with its clawed hands, shredding his clothes in the process. Arnold looked into the eyes of the beast and could see nothing but rage within them; this spirit beast had no control over what it was doing.

Feeling its warm breath on his face, Arnold felt like his fate was now out of his hands. If only he had been able to spirit wield. He heard the a shriek from his eagle as it clattered into the back of the beast, causing it to loosen its grip on Arnold. Sensing his opportunity, he managed to wriggle from its grasp and dropped onto the floor. Arnold kicked out at the beast's legs with as much strength as he could muster, causing it to topple to the floor. His eagle then took flight again, flying high up into the sky before turning and diving straight back down. It hurtled towards the beast, dive-bombing straight into it, sending a large dust cloud around them which made it difficult for Arnold to see.

When the dust eventually settled his eagle lay on the ground, its breathing laboured through exhaustion. Stood next to it was the beast. It seemed different now, calmer almost. It turned its head to Arnold. Its eyes stopped glowing and the green auro around it disappeared. The beast let out an ear-splitting roar before turning and running towards the far wall of the courtyard. Dropping to all fours, it quickly picked up the pace and vaulted over the wall. Just like that, the spirit beast was gone.

Dragging himself up from the floor, Arnold limped across to his eagle and crouched down next to it. He placed his hand on its side and a warm sensation came over him. The pain in his arm and throbbing in his back and sides began to subside as the eagle soothed his pain, its auro wrapping around him like a warm blanket. Behind him, he heard the storage container open.

"Arnold!" Everett cried as she ran over and wrapped herself around him. "Look at you, that was so stupid." She squeezed him tightly with tears streaming down her face from the stress of not knowing what was happening outside.

"Are you ok?" George put her hand out to help him to his feet.

"I'll be fine," he said, trying his hardest to play down his injuries. He grimaced as he climbed back to his feet.

"We need to get you checked over." Everett continued to examine Arnold, seeing his arm covered in blood.

"We can't hide this spirit beast from your dad, Arnold. He needs to know. What if it attacks someone else?" George was the rational one and Arnold had no choice but to agree with her. Everett and George stood on either side of him to help prop him up as his eagle began to dissipate back into him. "What was it?" George asked while struggling to help Arnold across the courtyard of the lockup.

"Like a wild animal. Whatever that spirit beast was it was not in control." A concerned look came across his face. "It looked…kind of human." Arnold realised how ridiculous that sounded but he was honestly more concerned with the fact that something about the beast felt familiar. Like a word on the tip of his tongue, it was something that Arnold could not quite put his finger on.

CHAPTER 8

"Where's my son?" Arnold could hear his mum outside the cubicle where he sat with Everett at the hospital.

"He's in bay 3, Mrs. Ethon," a nurse replied. His Mum pulled the curtains back from around the bay and let out a gasp as she saw Arnold battered and bruised, sat up in the hospital bed with his left arm bloodied. His Dad was stood beside her and looked equally concerned.

"Was this him? Was this Levent?" his dad asked. Mrs Ethon didn't wait for an answer and rushed over to Arnold, squeezing him tightly.

"Mum, you're hurting me. I'm ok!" he gasped, feeling as though he might lose consciousness if his mum hugged him any tighter. "I don't think it was. It couldn't have been?" Arnold said, answering his Dad's question. "It was like it was wild, Dad. I didn't see anyone around apart from the spirit beast. Is that even possible?"

"No, this doesn't make any sense. Why would it attack you?" his dad asked.

"I don't know. I just saw these wild green eyes and the way it moved around…" He paused for a moment, not wanting to sound like a delusional fool. "It was as though it was human."

"Human?" His Mum's tone raised as she spoke.

"I know it sounds crazy, but is that possible? It was a

spirit beast but, I don't know what kind. It was stood on two legs and had hands but with claws." He added the final part as he looked at the gash across the top of his arm.

"No, it's not," Arthur said, " but with everything that has happened recently I wouldn't rule anything out."

"Arnold was so brave. I dread to think what would have happened to us if he hadn't fought it off." Everett sat next to Arnold, her hand firmly grasping his as she spoke with pride. Arnold began to blush, feeling embarrassed at the fuss being made over him. A doctor walked in and explained that Arnold needed to have some stitches in his arm. Apart from that he just needed to rest for a couple of days and he would be fine. Once his arm had been stitched up, they left the hospital, dropping Everett off at home on the way. Once back home, Arnold hobbled up the stairs and entered his room before collapsing onto his bed, he felt exhausted. This was the most comfortable his bed had ever felt as Arnold felt himself drifting off to sleep

Arnold was at the tower. He wasn't flying, but he was high up on a branch of a nearby oak tree. He hadn't been here in his dreams for some time, but once he had got his bearings he soon felt accustomed to being in the form of an eagle. Arnold contemplated taking flight as he loved the exhilarating feeling of soaring in the sky and extending his wings. As he began to spread them, he felt a sharp stinging sensation within them. He drew them back in close to his body, the feeling knocking him sick. Arnold decided that he would remain perched on the tree rather than try flying as he didn't want to experience that shooting pain again. He padded his feet out as he got himself comfortable and began to take in the surroundings. He couldn't see much and he felt himself drifting off into a deeper sleep as he tucked his head into his chest, feeling exhausted.

Waking to the unwelcome noise from his alarm clock, Arnold felt as though he had only been asleep for a few moments when it had actually been seven hours. He could remember his dream and thought it strange that he had dreamed about being his eagle, realising that he had felt the pain it was experiencing from the fight with the spirit beast the day before. Arnold was convinced that when he was having these dreams, he was somehow connected to the spirit world. He slowly sat up in bed and realised he had slept in his ripped, dusty and blood-splattered clothes all night. He got undressed and jumped into the shower to freshen up. His arm was aching from both the slash received in the fight and the twelve stitches that he had subsequently had to patch him back up.

After his shower, he got himself dressed and ready for school before heading downstairs for breakfast. As he reached the bottom of the stairs, he saw that the ever eager paperboy had already been. The newspaper was sat on the doormat as neither his mum or dad had come downstairs yet. Arnold reached down for it to take to the dining table for his dad to read when he came down, most likely in the next few minutes.

The headline on the paper caught his attention immediately, the bold letters filling the top half of the paper. "The Beast of Oswald – Panic as local boy left fighting for life." Arnold stared at the headline, wondering at its inaccuracy; he was far from fighting for his life. He began to walk back to the dining table slowly, his gaze fixed on the newspaper article.

"A local boy has been left fighting for his life after being attacked by multiple murder suspect Levent. It is thought that the attack took place near the Bramley lock-up. It has left the boy in a critical condition after a frenzied encounter. Questions are being asked of the Chichen such as why did they fail to keep a member of the community safe from such an attack? Earlier this year Hershel Ethon, a retired Elder, was brutally murdered after the Chichen was unable to apprehend the threat known as Levent despite months of investigations. It is unknown at this time whether the victim will make it through the next few days. Questions need to be asked about the Chichen's ability to keep the town safe from this highly dangerous man. At the time of this story

breaking the Chichen has declined to comment."

Arnold continued to stare at the paper long after he finished reading the article. Whoever had written this had added two and two together and made ten. Not only was he ok, aside from some minor injuries that he knew he would recover from in the next week or two, but Levent had nothing to do with the attack. "Dad!" he shouted from the bottom of the stairs, uncertain of how his Dad would perceive the story. "There's something in the paper that I think you need to read." His Dad walked down the stairs with a curious look on his face, clearly intrigued as to what Arnold was alluding to.

"What is it?" he asked as he took the paper from Arnold's outstretched arm, unfolding the paper so that he could read it. He scanned the page momentarily. "What a load of rubbish," he sighed. "This is a way to create unrest against the Chichen. Who on earth has leaked that you were attacked? Not many people even know about it."

"It says the attack was Levent, but it wasn't. It was something worse." Arnold was concerned that the creature that attacked him was still on the loose. "What if it attacks someone else?"

"We have a lot of people out looking for it. There is no way that it won't be found and killed."

"Killed?" Arnold looked shocked at his dad's words. "What happened to capture not kill?"

"This thing is not human. It doesn't need capturing Arnold; it needs killing!"

"What if it is human?" asked Arnold.

"That is not possible, you have described it."

"Something doesn't seem right." Arnold spoke with certainty "There was something familiar about it, I don't know what, but I intend to find out."

"You need to keep away from this, Arnold. You are lucky to still be here."

"I managed to hold my own against it. I am still here because I could fight." Arnold's dad shook his head.

"Yes, you have grown stronger, but if not for your training this could have ended so differently. Don't go looking for the fight!" His Dad was not sugar-coating his advice.

"Who said anything about looking for a fight?" Arnold snapped back. "We need to find out who this is."

"Don't you mean what?" corrected his dad.

"No. Definitely who." With that, Arnold began to walk towards the front door, grabbing his back-pack from the side. As he threw his bag over his shoulder. He immediately regretted his cockiness as he winced at the discomfort from his injuries. He left the house and headed to school, well and truly confused as to what or who had attacked him and why.

Outside the weather was still warm, especially given the time of day it was. It felt unusual to keep experiencing the beautiful weather every morning. Arnold had opted not to wear his school blazer, which he had tucked between the straps of his bag. He continued his journey to school before stopping near the cenotaph to meet up with Everett. He could see from the top of the road that she stood waiting with George, courtesy of his enhanced vision. After a short while he had reached them, the sun beginning to heat his back. Everett spotted Arnold and ran over, throwing her arms around him before planting a kiss on his cheek. Arnold winced as she hugged him tightly, instantly going back in time to when Everett had embraced him for the first time last year after their encounter with Levent. He couldn't believe his luck that she was now his girlfriend, a fact that he had still not got used to and one that Otto had spent the whole of the last school year telling him would never happen.

"Sorry." Everett stepped back allowing Arnold to breathe, realising the discomfort he was clearly in. "How are you feeling?"

"I can't believe you are coming into school," George added. Despite the heat, she still insisted on wearing her favoured beanie hat.

"If I didn't come in, people would have started asking questions. Have you seen the paper this morning?"

"Yeah, how wrong have they got it. Levent wasn't even there. Do you think he had something to do with what happened?"

"Who knows? I do want to find out, though." Arnold spoke with conviction, clearly determined to get to the bottom of the mystery spirit beast.

"Where can we start?" Everett asked.

"With his dreams," George piped up. "We need to use his link to the spirit world to find him. We need to contact Levent."

CHAPTER 9

Arnold had not had any dreams about the spirit world for some time now. Not since he saw Levent and his Grandma at the tower, shortly after the murder of his Grandad. He had told Everett and George about the dream and he was adamant that his Grandma was still alive and trapped in the spirit world, where his Grandad had put her because of how dangerous she had become. The corruption from the dragon spirit beast had possessed her and she was no longer in control. Levent had thought that Arnold's spirit beast was also a dragon and had planned to exploit Arnold's anger and hatred for him to let it manifest in this form, allowing him to take it for himself. Levent was a menial and so he didn't possess his own spirit beast. But he had a blade that would allow him to take someone else's and use it as his own.

His grandad had merely been collateral, just a pawn in Levent's twisted game. Even worse was the revelation that he was Arnold's uncle and the ease with which Levent had killed his own dad still appalled him. The hatred that Arnold felt for Levent was eating him up on the inside. Arnold hated him so much for what he had taken from him and dreaded to think how he would react should he come face to face with his uncle once more. As for his Grandma, she had been put in the spirit world for a reason. He had no intention of exploring how she was still there and how she had not aged a day since being trapped there.

"You want me to use my connection to the spirit world to contact Levent?" Arnold was not impressed with George's idea one bit.

"Hear me out."

"I haven't got time for this." With that, Arnold began to set off towards school. He had no intention of making any contact with Levent.

"Arnold!" Everett scolded him. "There's no need to be like that with George! She is only trying to help." Arnold stopped walking to allow George to finish her sentence, albeit reluctantly.

"You saw them and they saw you." George was referring to his last dream where his Grandma appeared to shift her gaze directly towards Arnold. "She interacted with you being in the surrounding area. What if you can do the same?" To give her credit, George had a point and Arnold did agree that if his grandma was able to spot him in a dream then maybe he would be able to interact with them when he was in his dream, too. From what Arnold could tell, somehow when asleep he was linking with his eagle spirit beast within the spirit world and seeing through its eyes, feeling what it was feeling and sometimes controlling its movements. He had always believed these were just dreams. After his last experience, Arnold was more than confident that he was directly connecting to the spirit world. Something that neither he nor his friends had ever heard of.

"Even if I wanted to contact them, which I don't by the way, I haven't had any dreams about flying for the last three months." He wasn't lying; the dreams had stopped abruptly. Although he missed dreaming of that sensation of flying, he didn't want to come face to face with Levent or his Grandma given everything that had happened. Deep down Arnold knew he would be happy if he never saw either of them again.

"That is where we need to start then, how do we get you to the spirit world again?" Arnold knew that George was on to something and decided to follow her idea, given that they had absolutely nothing else to go on. "Any ideas about how we are going to do that?"

"I will look into it," George replied. "I will ask my Granny at lunchtime."

George's Granny had an old shop in town that specialised in traditional herbs and remedies. George was close to her Granny; she spent most of her spare time with her. She either helped her at home or assisted her in her shop. George loved reading and researching, so this latest idea was right up her street.

"This can't be a good idea." Everett stood between them, not impressed with the plan. "It's a crazy idea to go looking for Levent."

"It's an idea though and at least it gives us something to aim for." Arnold dreaded the thought of coming face to face with Levent again, but at this moment in time, he felt it was the only option. "George, let me know as soon as you find anything that can help."

The three of them continued their journey to school. Arnold couldn't help but feel that at some point their plan was going to backfire on them. However, he also felt he had a responsibility to locate whatever it was that attacked him at the lock-up. Arnold needed to do this before anyone else got hurt, or it came after him again. He knew school was getting in the way, but he also knew that if he didn't go there, his dad would not allow him to go to the Chichen to train. They reached the school grounds and its usual early morning mayhem with other students rushing back and forth. There were those trying to make sure they were in on time as well as those who stood huddled in groups, catching up on the latest gossip. Arnold walked in as casually as ever to not draw attention to the injuries that lay hidden under his uniform.

After leaving Everett and George, Arnold made his way down the winding corridors, exiting one building to take a shortcut he knew. It was a pathway not meant for students but he often made the shortcut without anyone noticing.

"Ethon!" He heard the voice from behind him and he recognised the Scottish accent straight away. He knew that it was Peter, with Gary and Dave stood at either side of him. "Ethon!" Peter called again.

"What now?" Arnold snapped back. He absolutely wasn't in the mood for this.

"Where's your boar friend?" Peter sneered. "Not around to fight your battles?"

"Last time I saw you, I saw you receive that cut to your nose. Do you want to see what would happen if it was me punching you?" Arnold could not stand Peter and having discovered a newfound confidence in his abilities meant that he did not feel intimidated by him anymore.

"Except you haven't got your boar friend or Otto to protect you like you usually have. You're all alone. No one else around except you and us." He stepped into Arnold's personal space in an attempt to intimidate him. Arnold grinned, trying to keep his calm and refusing to move. He was stronger than he had ever been and was not going to be easily pushed around this year.

"Something funny, Ethon?" Peter growled, less than impressed with Arnold.

"Not really. Just your nose looks even funnier this close up." Gary and Dave sniggered from behind Peter and his face became contorted with anger, he pushed Arnold backwards. Arnold tried to stand his ground but grimaced with the pain that shot down his side courtesy of the heavy bruising he had sustained in the attack with the creature. Arnold steadied himself and stepped forward towards Peter but found Gary and Dave at either side of him, restraining his arms. Peter grinned and stepped forward, aiming a blow to Arnold's side.

"This should knock you down a peg." He growled as he

continued to volley punches at Arnold.

"Stop!" Arnold begged, his sides aching. He tried to loosen his arms, but Gary and Dave had a firm hold of them both.

Peter laughed "Is this all you have? You may be able to talk it but let's face it - you are still just as pathetic." He stepped forward again to throw down further blows on Arnold's body. Arnold used Gary and Dave's weight to lift his legs from the ground and kick Peter backwards away from him, knocking him to the floor in the process. He then used his momentum by swinging his legs back to the floor and pulled Gary and Dave together in front of him before starting to exchange blows with the two of them. Gary swung a haymaker at him, but Arnold quickly maneuvered himself out of the way and pushed him with force backwards towards Peter, knocking the two of them over in the process. Dave looked at Arnold and attempted to land a punch on him, but again Arnold dodged the intended blow with ease given that Dave's large frame meant he was considerably slower than Arnold was. Arnold stepped forward and landed a blow across Dave's face, knocking him straight to the floor.

Peter climbed back to his feet and ran at Arnold, spearing him to the floor and knocking the wind out of him in the process. Arnold knew he was stronger than the three of them, but he was carrying injuries that were limiting what he could do. His body was throbbing as Peter began to thump down on his body. He was determined to prove a point to Arnold. Peter was raining blows on his body and not his face. Peter swung both arms in the air to slam these down on Arnold but found himself slammed into the floor. Arnold looked across to see Marrok stood there with his arm outstretched. "Need a hand?" he smiled. Grabbing his arm, Arnold pulled himself back to his feet.

"Now three against one isn't really fair." Marrok spoke with an air of arrogance as he walked over to Peter and kicked him in the side, knocking him back to the floor before rolling him towards his heavies who also lay sprawled out on the floor. "But three against two? I like those odds." He smirked at Peter. Peter was furious and jumped back to his feet "Come on, then," he growled.

"What on earth is going on here?!" a voice called from the doorway. It was Mr. Higgins, head of technology. "Follow me, now. All of you." They all scowled but did as they were told and followed Mr. Higgins across the courtyard. Arnold knew straight away that they were being marched to their head of year's office. He dragged Peter, Gary and Dave in first instructing Arnold and Marrok to sit on the chairs outside.

"Listen," Marrok said under his breath. "I know how the Chichen works. If you get in trouble for fighting here, you will be punished there too."

"I can't let you take the blame."

"I'm the new kid. After this, everyone will leave me alone and you don't get reprimanded at the Chichen. Win-win, really. Just follow my lead. Ok?" It didn't sit well with Arnold, but he felt that Marrok was giving him little choice in the matter. The office door opened and Peter and his goons scurried out of the office. Next, Mr. Higgins led them away to another room.

"You two in here, please." Mrs. Elctree's stern voice was intimidating. "Sit there." She gestured to the chairs on the other side of her desk and sat forward with her fingers interlocked. Her glasses perched on the end of her pointed nose. "Tell me what happened."

"They jumped Arnold, Miss. I got there and the three of them were beating him up. So, I ended it." Marrok spoke before Arnold had the chance to say anything.

"So you're saying you caused all three of their injuries because they were beating Arnold up?" She turned to face him. "Is this true?" Arnold didn't know what to say, so he simply nodded in agreement even though this didn't feel right to him. "Fighting is forbidden at this school, whether justified in your eyes or not so I'm sorry Marrok, I am going to have to call your mum as you are suspended for the rest of the week. The same goes for Peter, Gary and Dave." She pushed her glasses back up her nose before continuing. "Arnold, may I suggest you go back to class? That is if you are ok to do so?" Sensing an opportunity, Arnold played on his injuries and groaned a little. "My side is sore miss."

"Very well, you should take the rest of the day off to rest. I will contact your parents." Arnold stood up and made his way out of the office. Glancing at Marrok, he noticed he was discreetly giving him the thumbs up. Arnold knew he now had the rest of the day to look into the creature that attacked him, time he planned on using effectively. First, though, Arnold wanted to get home and lie down given that the throbbing in his sides had intensified given his latest scuffle.

After getting the ok from Mrs. Elctree, Arnold headed home and lay on his bed. He felt battered and bruised and he just wanted to relax. His brain, however, could not switch off. He spent the rest of the morning laid out on his bed, scrolling through various apps on his phone.

As he lay staring at his screen, a text came through from George.

"Heard that you got sent home. I'm at Granny's shop as planned. You should come here. G x."

He had been staring at his phone but had not realised that it was lunchtime and George was well underway with her plan. Quickly getting changed out of his uniform, Arnold headed across town to meet George at her Granny's herbal remedies shop.

The shop was just a ten-minute walk from his house and when Arnold reached it, he could see George leaning against the counter while talking to her Granny. His enhanced vision was working despite the windows looking like they needed a good clean. The sign above the window read 'Rushton's Remedies'. Arnold often wondered how the shop managed to stay open at times given that not many people seemed to go in to buy things. However, Arnold knew George's Granny also practised as a healer and thought now would be an excellent time to see if she could do anything to help him with his aching body.

Waiting for a gap in the passing cars, he bided his time before deciding to make a quick bolt across the road, growing impatient with waiting. He walked through the wooden framed door and heard a bell ring. George and her Granny looked across straight away with George flashing him a smile when she realised it was him.

"How are you? I heard what happened. As if they suspended Marrok," she said, walking towards him.

"I'm fine, just a little achy. I should have been suspended, too but Marrok took the fall. He insisted on it." George's Granny stood with her back turned to both of them. Arnold could see her moving her hands and there was what looked like steam or smoke rising in front of her, casting a perfumed smell around the room. She leaned over slowly to pull out a chalice which she then placed on the worktop. Her arched back was reflective of her age, given that she was George's great Grandma and had been running the shop for over fifty years. Her white permed hair showed that she still took pride in her appearance and it complimented the dark floral dress that she was wearing. She ground up some herbs in a pestle and mortar and then added them to another bowl in front of her. Next, she reached for a ladle from the rack above her using a small step that she could move around the shop to help her reach things. Using the ladle, she scooped a liquid from the bowl and transferred this to the chalice. She turned and walked out from around the counter and over to Arnold.

"Here, drink this dear." She held out the mixture for him to take.

Reluctantly he accepted. It looked awful, smelt like flowers and Arnold could still not decide whether it was smoke or steam that was coming from it. However, he politely took the drink, choosing to drink it as quickly as possible. He didn't catch the taste of the drink until three large gulps in and he gagged as he struggled to finish it; it tasted how it looked.

George's Granny smiled. "What did you expect? Cola?" she laughed. "That's a family remedy that my mum taught me when I was just a young girl. Tastes terrible, but those aches and pains you are feeling will subside soon, I promise." It was telling how much Arnold trusted her, given that he had just drunk the vile liquid without even asking what it was first. "Georgina tells me you can connect with the spirit world through your dreams," she said as she walked back around to the other side of the counter. "Very rare indeed, if it's true." Arnold nodded.

"I used to have dreams that I was flying. Then my spirit beast turned out to be an eagle. Since then, my dreams have stopped."

"I see. It may be that now the connection is complete there is no need for these dreams or visions." She began to potter about picking up different herbs and remedies and putting them into a fresh bowl. "It might be that you just experienced dreams. However, if there is a true connection you need to be very careful not to interact with anything on the other side." The tone of her voice changed as she continued to grind and add herbs to her latest remedy. "If you interact with something that is in the spirit world, you run the risk of it trapping you there." Knowing their plan was to contact Levent in the spirit world, he felt uncomfortable keeping it from George's Granny. "We won't." George cut him off before he continued.

"We just want to see if it is a dream or if it is a connection." Arnold was surprised at George given how close she was with her Granny. If Arnold felt unsure about contacting Levent, he felt even more uneasy now that he had been forewarned he could get trapped in the spirit world.

George's Granny cast her a look that implied that she didn't fully believe the words that had just come out of her grandaughter's mouth. "I trust you, Georgina."

"George, Granny," she corrected.

"That is not the name you were given at birth. It's not the name I will be using for you." She finished what she was doing and poured the fine powder that she had created into a little brown bag before sealing it and passing it to Arnold. "Here you go. Just add some boiling water before you go to sleep and inhale the vapours that it produces. If there is a connection, you will know about it by the time you wake up."

"Thank you." Arnold felt grateful for the remedies that George's Granny had given him, the one he had already drank earlier must have kicked in as he already felt his aches subsiding. George's Granny simply smiled and began to potter around the shop.

"You're going to be late back, Georgina." George checked her phone and realised she needed to get back to school, sharpish. "It's a start, walk me back to school?"

As requested, Arnold walked her back to school and saw her off at the gates before heading back to his house with the powder that her Granny had given him. He planned to follow her instructions and use the powder before going to sleep that night. All he had to do now was clock watch until the rest of the day passed away.

CHAPTER 10

It had been a long and tedious afternoon and evening with Arnold sat on his bed, staring at his clock. Granny's remedy had worked wonders and he felt so much better for drinking it. What it didn't help with was the lecture he had received from his parents once they had got home regarding his fight at school. Even if the school had believed Marrok his parents were not daft and knew that Arnold had been more involved. He could still hear his dad's patronising voice, reminding him that he needed to walk away from those situations given his increased physical abilities. He understood what his dad was saying but it had felt so good to show Peter and his goons that they couldn't push him around anymore. He felt guilty about Marrok being suspended when he was really at fault but Marrok had been right; he would have received a further reprimand by the Chichen for fighting.

Finally, it was half-past nine and Arnold headed downstairs with the powder he had been given and headed to the kitchen to switch on the kettle. He put a bowl on the side and poured the powder out of the little brown bag before adding the freshly boiled water and stirring it in. Arnold grabbed a tea towel and placed this underneath to avoid burning his hands before carrying it upstairs. Once in his room, he placed the bowl on top of his drawers. He put his head over the top of the bowl and breathed in deeply, taking in the vapours as George's granny had instructed. The vapour smell was inviting; Arnold thought it resembled parma violet sweets. On the first inhale, the steam scalded his throat. The breaths he took in after this were more steady to avoid this happening again.

After a few minutes, the vapour began to fade as the liquid cooled. Taking this as a sign he had inhaled enough, Arnold stepped away and went and sat on his bed and waited for something to happen. He didn't feel any different but then he didn't really know what to expect. Arnold lay down on his bed and before he knew it, he had drifted off into the deepest sleep.

He was soaring high, the sensation of being this high up just as exhilarating as before. He had missed that unique chill from the wind as it pushed back against his feathers, the vibrations soothing the strain he felt from the wings keeping him in flight. Looking down, he could see the shimmer from the sun reflecting on the lake beneath him. He saw the pine trees around it and the familiar mountain range and immediately he knew that he recognised the area. He changed his flight path accordingly and began to fly in the direction of the tower, which lay just beyond the mountains in front of him.

He had missed this feeling and wow did it feel good. He felt free up here, invincible as though nothing could touch him. At this moment, with this feeling, he wished he could stay like this. The picturesque landscape was like something you would see in the most detailed oil painting. It was so beautiful it didn't seem real. He rode wave after wave of wind, further developing his gliding ability, something he was beginning to master. Rising high in the sky he would dip suddenly, the rush of which would spike his adrenaline before using the pressurised force to push himself higher in the air before dropping again. He repeated this process over and over until eventually, he could see a familiar building in the distance at the top of a hill. It was the tower where he last saw Levent and his grandma talking. When she had seen Arnold perched on a tree, listening in on their conversation.

He wondered if they would both be there. He then wondered how he would communicate with them, he was currently in the form of an eagle and last time he checked eagles could not talk. Gliding gracefully, Arnold landed on the window ledge and peered through the window, looking for a sign that someone was around.

Then he saw him, moving around through a doorway at the far corner of the room.

Arnold glided further around the tower to land on another window ledge, he was aiming to get a better look at Levent. Standing with his overcoat removed and wearing a black tank top, he was laid out on the floor doing press-ups. He must have been training for a while given the amount of sweat that was pouring off him. His focus appeared undeterred. After around five minutes he stopped to take a rest, walking over to a table to pick up a glass of water and taking a drink before placing it back down. His face had the same look of anger he recognised etched on it. Arnold wondered if this look was permanently fixed to his face.

Slowly beneath the anger a crooked smile overcame Levent's face. Then his eyes changed their path and settled on Arnold. Arnolds heart sank; Levent had noticed him and Arnold had not thought about what to do next.

Levent began to walk slowly towards the window. "There you are," he purred. "I wondered when you would come back again." His voice was as menacing as ever, a hostile undertone to his words. Arnold panicked and jumped backwards, quickly realising that there was no hard surface behind him. Arnold had been perched on the window ledge and he promptly flapped his wings to regain his balance and stop himself from falling. Levent gestured for Arnold to come in through the partially opened window. "You have come a lot closer than you did last time I saw you here. Either you are feeling a lot more confident, or you are here to confront me." His wild grin intensified at the thought of a confrontation. Arnold had not come here to fight; however, he wanted to talk but could not in this form. He didn't trust Levent at all and knew if he stepped through the window that he would be in his environment and there would be a high chance that he would not get out again. Having had the displeasure of being trapped in the basement within the tower when he was kidnapped by Sue just a few months earlier, he knew deep down that he never wanted to step foot within those stone walls again.

Having no other way to communicate, Arnold began to tap over and over on the window. He moved his head in the direction away from the tower. Levent just began laughing "No!" he hissed angered at being told what to do by Arnold. "You should know you can be trapped here." He echoed the warning that he had heard earlier from George's granny. "That wouldn't be of any use to me. I have a bigger plan for you." Levent turned around and began training once more. "She, however…" He looked over his shoulder at Arnold.

Noticing the large shadow that was forming around him, Arnold spun round to see a large dark creature hurtling towards him at speed. Not having much time to take in any details apart from the large, intimidating wingspan of the creature before him, Arnold dropped from the ledge and then stretched out his wings to glide up into the air, flying past the dark creature at speed as their trajectories crossed. His heart was pounding, another moment later and who knows what would have happened to him. He continued to fly as fast as he could; he didn't even want to think what would happen if the spirit beast behind him were to catch him up.

He didn't look behind. He just kept flying as fast and as hard as he could towards the mountains. The wind, however, was not helping him. It felt like it was pushing against him with so much force that he quickly lost the momentum that he had gained. He decided he had to turn slightly and use the power from the wind rather than fighting against it and seeing a pine forest not too far from him, he decided that would be his best chance for cover. He reached the wooded area quickly and flew between the trees at speed, not waiting to see if the monstrous creature was close behind him. He soon realised that he had flown in too fast. He narrowly managed to dodge one tree before clipping his wing against the branch of another and came crashing down to the ground at speed.

Arnold sat bolt upright in bed. Cold sweat was pouring from his face and he knew straight away that his experience had been far too close for comfort and he did not want to do that again any time soon. He had interacted with Levent in the spirit world and narrowly escaped from what he presumed was his grandma's dragon spirit beast. His chest was pounding and his breathing was heavy. He began to breathe through his nose to slow his breathing back down to a steady pace before heading to the bathroom to wash his face. After getting a glass of water from downstairs, Arnold returned to his bedroom and lay back down on his bed. He glanced across at his clock, it was half-past four in the morning. Arnold did not go back to sleep for fear of crossing back over to the spirit world or more precisely, for fear of what would happen if he came across his grandma once more.

Levent had said he had a bigger plan for Arnold and as he lay sleepless for the next two hours, his mind racing, he wondered what exactly that could mean.

CHAPTER 11

"Never again!" Arnold spoke with conviction as he headed to school with Everett and George.

"You look shattered," Everett said, holding Arnold's hand tightly.

"Granny did warn you," George added.

"He said he has a bigger plan for me and that he had no intention of trapping me in the spirit world," Arnold recalled. "He also said he hadn't seen me since my grandma spotted me three months ago, so I don't think he has anything to do with the creature that attacked me."

"Don't forget that he has an army of menials out there, Arnold," Everett highlighted. "He could just as easily be getting one of them to do his dirty work. Like he did with that receptionist at your Chichen." Arnold knew that Everett was right; he could be getting one of his menials to attack him with the use of an artefact. However, deep down, he just didn't believe it.

"What now?" George asked. "We haven't got anything to go off."

"I have a feeling that he will be paying a visit soon," Arnold suggested. "Levent said he has a bigger plan for me.

As I'm not going back to the spirit world, I reckon it's only a matter of time before he comes to me."

"That's a dangerous game to play, Arnold," Everett said, her face full of concern. "Don't forget this guy has murdered people."

"I don't need reminding, thank you!" Arnold snapped. A sad-looking Everett let go of Arnold's hand as they continued their journey. Arnold was quick to apologise. "Sorry, I didn't mean to be rude."

"It's ok, but you need to realise you can't bite everyone's head off every time they mention your grandad." Arnold knew what Everett was talking about. However, he couldn't help but feel the rush of anger that overcame him every time he thought about what Levent had done to his grandad. Arnold had been tied up and made to witness Levent and his Grandad in combat with one another. His Grandad was surprisingly strong and was able to hold his own against Levent and his two giant lion spirit beasts, even managing to fell one of the lions during the battle. This was when Levent had made the revelation that his Grandad had trapped his Grandma in the spirit world when her dragon spirit beast had corrupted her. Levent also dropped the bombshell that she was pregnant with him at the time meaning he had grown up in the spirit world and had somehow managed to find a way to travel between there and the real world.

Arnold's stomach churned as he thought about being powerless from stopping Levent when he buried his blade into his Grandad. The anger it caused him gave him the strength to break free and harness the power of his eagle spirit beast. If only he had been able to summon it just a few seconds sooner. Maybe his grandad would still be alive. H would still around to go and talk to about his worries, to wind him up about his girlfriend. He just wanted to spend time with him again regardless of what they were doing. But he was gone and he wasn't ever coming back. Being part of the Chichen meant that Arnold knew that he had to abide by their laws, meaning that if he were to take Levent's life in revenge, he would be kicked out. He knew that if he were to honour his Grandad and remain at the Chichen, Arnold would only be allowed to capture Levent as this was the way that he had been trained. After all, Otto was thrown out for taking Sue's life, even though that was done in self-defence.

The three of them made it to school and Arnold discovered that he had a pretty dull day. After the events of the last few days, it was something of a relief. He blocked out his worries and worked hard through all of his classes to try and take his mind off everything. He soon reached the end of the day and while all the other students were now packing up to head home, Arnold knew that he would be heading to the Chichen to train. No amount of aching body parts would stop him from attending. Arnold loved every second of being involved at the Chichen and found the physical aspects of training a great way of relieving any stress or frustration he was feeling. This was why he had trained so hard over the summer; to try and focus his anger about his Grandad and do something productive with it.

Arnold walked by the canal that ran down the side of Oswald and couldn't help but admire the old abandoned factories that followed the other side of the canal in its entirety. Back in the day, Oswald had been front and centre for various trades, given its convenient location. It had access to land and the ability to join onto the canal that headed to Leeds one way and Liverpool on the other. The factories were ideal points for manufacturing things such as cotton, as they could be traded between the two cities which maximised profits. Oswald's other major source of income had been the coal mines that ran deep below the town. However, after the mining strikes, the tunnels became disused. Over time they were completely abandoned with traders finding it cheaper to import from overseas. This led to the decline in trade and over time, every factory was shut down. All that stood now were nothing more than empty shells around the town. A reminder of the success the town had once had. Arnold imagined what it must have looked like when everything was running how it should be and felt sad to see all the smashed windows and graffiti-covered walls that were left behind. He carried on his walk up the canal and cut across a small bridge and made his way up the entrance of the Chichen and through the large oak door.

As he arrived, he could see that the new receptionist was busy typing away. He surveyed the area to try and figure out where he should go. His body was telling him to head to the athenium and do some reading rather than physical training. His head, however, had a different idea. He followed the checkerboard floor to his left and put his finger on the pressure pad next to the training room and waited for it to bleep to give him access. Once it did, he quickly got himself dressed into his training robes and headed across to the weapons room to take out his Grandad's Macuahuitl. He had been training with this weapon for a good three months now. He picked it up and began to move it slowly through the air as he reminded himself of its weight and how best to balance when wielding it. Unlike most weapons, the Macuahuitl was heaviest at its hilt, making it quite tricky to balance. Arnold had found that he was slowly getting used to judging how to best use it. He looked at the intricate carvings decorated on both sides of the ancient weapon. His Grandad had acquired it when he was younger and while still working as a Doyen for the Chichen.

Arnold held the blade in both hands as it made it easier to move and began to move backwards and forwards while practising different stances that his dad had been teaching him. He spent around half an hour honing his defensive poses and blocks before spending the next thirty minutes practising his offensive strikes and stances before stopping for a short break. Arnold walked across to his bag and pulled out a bottle of water and took a gulp to clench his thirst before grabbing his towel and padding his face with it. He had been training well and hard and his training robes were beginning to dampen from his sweat.

Arnold heard the bleep from the keypad and knew someone was coming into the training room. Arnold turned to see who it was. His dad walked in, also dressed in his training robes and walked across the room. "Training hard, I see," he smiled. "The athenium would have been a better choice given your recent fights, but I knew you would be in here. You're just like him."

"I don't think sticking my head in a book would help me at the moment. I need to focus. I need to be ready in case that thing comes after me again."

"I understand son, but sooner or later you are going to have to let your body rest," his dad advised. He began rummaging around in the weapons room before coming back out with two weapon hilts, neither with a weapon attached to them. "Put the Macuahuitl down. We need to train with these for the time being." Arnold cast a sceptical look in his dad's direction, thinking that he had overworked himself and was beginning to lose the plot.

"Er, I'm not being funny, dad, but how are we meant to train with them?"

"The other day at school, you shot an arrow using energy directly from the spirit world." Arnold shrugged.

"Yeah. Marrok said it's called spirit wielding." His dad nodded.

"This is a rare skill, Arnold and one that your Grandad possessed." He passed one of the hilts to his son and held firmly on to the other. He then began to focus on the hilt and pointed the open palm of his other hand in its direction, placing it over the end of the hilt. He closed his eyes momentarily and his hand began to glow a soft blue colour, which was his dad's auro. He then pulled his open palm away from the hilt and as he did this, he appeared to leave a bright light behind. When he pulled his hand away fully, he revealed a spirit blade that was now emanating from the hilt of the sword. Arnold stood there awestruck, sure that what he had just witnessed was one of the coolest things he had ever seen.

"How?" he asked.

"With practice and lots of it." Arnold smiled. The blade matched the colour of his dad's auro. It didn't flicker, but it was transparent; he could see right through the blade. Arnold could feel the power and the energy emitting from the blade as it ruffled both their clothes as if the wind was blowing them. The force felt incredible and reminded Arnold of the sensation he felt against his feathers when he was flying. It wasn't the wind; it was spirit energy.

"Is it-?"Arnold began. His dad tapped the blade against the floor and it made a clinking noise, confirming to Arnold that the blade was physically present.

"You managed to fire an arrow with raw spirit energy, totally unharnessed. That shows the powerful connection you have to the spirit world. In that raw state, however, you could have caused more damage to the surrounding area. It is important that I teach you how to spirit wield safely." His dad opened his free palm once more and it began to glow with his blue auro. He pressed his palm against the top of the blade back down to the hilt. As if pressing the blade back, just like that, the blade was gone. "Before we get started, you need to know how these weapon artefacts work," he began. "They help harness the energy from the spirit world and assist you with spirit wielding."

"If that's the case, how did I do it from a bow at school?" Arnold asked.

"You fired an arrow using pure energy. This is not something that is known to happen without the use of a weapon artefact. It's why I need to train you on how to harness this ability safely. You don't want to inadvertently hurt yourself or others." Walking to the other side of the room, he placed the hilt on a bench. "To begin with, you need to learn to focus your auro." Arnold felt up for the challenge so stood opposite his dad and mimicked his stance. He closed his eyes and awaited instruction. "You need to focus on your spirit beast. Focus on its power and the energy that it creates." Arnold felt like he did when he meditated with Mr. Whittaker and found his eagle for the first time. He followed the instructions and began to focus on his spirit beast until he felt a surge inside; he knew from the feeling that he had linked with his spirit beast. He nodded at his dad to tell him that he had connected with his eagle. "That is the easy part. This next part is where you need to practice. Now you need to focus on the trait that your spirit beast intensifies."

Arnold was momentarily confused. "What do you mean?" he asked.

"Keep focused, Arnold. Think to when you summoned your eagle for the first time. The feelings you experienced are what triggered your connection and finally enabled you to become one with it." Arnold went back to when he summoned it for the first time and again felt a surge of anger, thinking back to being tied up while his grandad's life ended. No sooner did he feel the rush of anger than he was disabled with what felt like an electric shock. He dropped flat to the floor, his muscles feeling as though they had all tightened up, as though he had an all-body cramp. It was horrendous and Arnold cried out as he lay in pain on the floor.

His dad stood over him. "Break your connection, Arnold!" Arnold was trying but continued to writhe on the floor in agony, the pain so immense he could not break the connection. He didn't know how to; it was though he was stuck to it and unable to break free from the raw energy from the spirit world. Seeing that he was struggling his dad knelt and grabbed hold of Arnold. "Accept the energy that is coursing through you. You need to learn to harness it. Look at me, accept that pain, Arnold." Arnold opened his eyes and looked at his dad, but it was too difficult and his body continued to convulse. He didn't know how much longer he could stand this for. After a few moments, his dad's words became increasingly muffled as he slipped into unconsciousness.

When he woke, he was unsure how long he had been

unconscious but what he did know was that his body was aching all over.

"Here, drink this." His dad passed him a drink that looked and had an aroma similar to the remedy George's granny had given him. Arnold sat up and accepted the drink. Remembering the foul taste he drank it in one. "Let's try again." His dad pressed.

"What?!" Arnold said, alarmed at what was being asked of him.

"I told you this wasn't going to be easy. You need to develop your strength so you can maintain that energy without crumpling to the floor like you just did." He didn't like the idea of going through all that again but understood that to get stronger, he absolutely needed to. He reluctantly climbed back to his feet and gathered himself.

"Let's go again" His Dad ordered.

Arnold knew that this was going to take everything he had to master this new skill.

CHAPTER 12

Arnold spent the next two weeks settling into the new school year. After having a rough start, he was intent on getting his head down and keeping a low profile. Everything seemed to have settled down following his fight with Peter and his goons with Peter opting to leave him alone for the time being. News soon spread about him taking on all three of the boys himself and Arnold had become pretty popular as a result. Marrok's plan had definitely worked. He hadn't had any more dreams, nor did he want to after his last experience, to the point where Arnold was struggling to get to sleep at times for worrying about accidentally slipping across to the spirit world.

What he had been doing was training intently at the Chichen every night to further hone his skills around spirit wielding. So far, however, he had spent most of his time violently convulsing on the floor with raw energy from the spirit world surging through him. His dad had told him that it would be sometime before he was able to channel this effectively. Every night he would do as his dad instructed and focus on what he felt when his grandad had died. Every time he did this however, his body could not cope with his auro. It would leave him a groaning heap on the floor, much to his dad's amusement. Arnold however, was determined to succeed, no matter how painful or embarrassing the process was. He was determined to keep trying until he was able to harness this power. The main reason for him wanting this ability was to use it against the unknown creature should it attack him again. Arnold had racked his brain to figure out where it had come from but the only person he could think of was Levent. However, his story about remaining in the spirit world seemed legitimate and Arnold believed him.

Arnold picked himself up from the floor in the training room after trying one last time for the night. Knowing his body was at its maximum for pain and feeling as though he could vomit at any moment, he quickly reached for his water bottle for a drink. Arnold took a seat on the bench at the side of the room while gathering his breath, sweat dripping down his face. After a short break, he packed up his bag and exited the training room for the night, walking ever so gingerly down the corridor thanks to his aching muscles. He was getting used to the aching now, but it did not mean that it hurt any less; his pain threshold was increasing. It was later than usual when he left that evening. Looking out from one of the windows, he could see that the sun had begun to set and his rumbling stomach reminded him that he was still yet to eat anything substantial. He could already hear the lecture his mum would give him when he finally returned home.

His dad hadn't been at the Chichen this evening, having informed Arnold that he had a meeting to attend outside of town. This meant Arnold had been on his own for the last three hours. Making it to the bottom of the corridor, he began to hear an echoed conversation coming from the offices. Initially, Arnold didn't think anything of it but then he recognised one of the voices. It was the voice that had scolded him when he called around at Otto's to talk to him; Mayor Redburn. He also knew the other voice he could hear was Mr. Whittaker's.

"I will ensure that no one asks any questions." Mr.

Whittaker's words echoed down the corridor and bounced around the main lobby in surprising fashion. Arnold stopped in his tracks, intrigued by what he had just heard. He decided to loiter around for a while to listen to what was being discussed. Arnold felt that they must have thought that the Chichen was empty, given how brazenly they were both talking.

"I appreciate that. Remember this will benefit both of us," Mayor Redburn responded. "People will start to whisper if they knew. The last thing we want is the paper to get wind of it and cause a panic."

"I would suggest that you take care of this operation, Mayor Redburn. I trust that if you are successful, I will be the first to know."

"Don't worry. As soon as we get access to the coal mine, you will know. It's only a matter of time."

The coal mine? Arnold was immediately confused, why after being shut for over forty years would they be looking to re-open the mines. Especially given the risk to the surrounding houses that the old mine shafts ran beneath. Arnold made for the door quietly, trying his hardest not to let his trainers squeak on the finely polished floor. Reaching for the front door he opened it slowly and exited the Chichen. 'Access to the coal mine?' he thought to himself once more as he walked down the steps of the Chichen and back down to the main road. No wonder they don't want the papers to get hold of the story.

Arnold was not Mr. Whittaker's biggest fan however he thought that Mayor Redburn hated him, given that he had thrown Otto out of the Chichen with no chance of ever returning, exiled like he was a traitor or a criminal. Arnold was surprised that he had heard the two of them in the same room, never mind making plans to work with each other. He knew that the coal mines didn't have anything to do with him, but he couldn't help but think of those it could seriously affect. He continued his journey home, trying to think why they would want to re-open the mine. Arnold just couldn't work it out.

Making the short journey home, he hung his bag up in the porch before heading into the kitchen to see what his mum had prepared for tea. It was enchiladas. Checking the temperature, he knew they must have been there a while and so he put them into the microwave to heat them up. He stood there waiting patiently while the microwave continued to make its loud humming noise, waiting for the three loud beeps to sound. When they were ready, he placed them on a plate and moved through to the dining room to tuck in, the smell making Arnold even more hungry than he was before.

"You should start getting back at a decent time." He had been waiting for his mum to surface and begin his lecture about making sure he was eating correctly to keep his energy levels up. He sat at the table and started to tuck in, making his way through the cheese-covered delights at an impressive rate. "Slow down. You will give yourself indigestion." Arnold took the advice and slowed down, not wanting any more lectures.

"Sorry, mum, I didn't realise what the time was."

"You have been at the Chichen a lot this week. Maybe have a rest tomorrow?"

"We'll see," Arnold responded, knowing that he had no intention of having a day off. "There is one thing."

"What's that?"

"The coal mines. What area do they run underneath?"

"Why?" his mum asked, apparently puzzled by the random question. At this point, the front door opened and Arnold's dad walked into the dining room.

"What are you guys talking about?" he asked, his weary face showing the signs of tiredness from his busy day at work.

"Arnold was just asking me about the coal mines," his mum explained.

"Why?" His dad's tone appeared more suspicious than his mum's.

"Er..." Arnold stuttered not knowing if he should disclose the conversation he had overheard. "I heard Mayor Redburn and Mr. Whittaker talking about the coal mines. I think Mayor Redburn wants to re-open them."

"He can't!" Judging by his reaction, Arnold knew straight away that his dad didn't know anything about the deal he had overheard being struck. "What do you mean?" he pressed, wanting to know more from him. "Those mines were closed for a reason and they should stay closed. They need to stay closed." He pulled out his phone and started dialling a number.

Arnold panicked. If his dad called Mr. Whittaker, he would know that he must have overheard them as no one else was around. "No dad, they don't know I heard. You can't say anything."

"Pardon?"

"I overheard them talking. If you tell them you know about the mines, they will know it was me." His dad paused.

"Ok, I wouldn't want that. I will see if Mr. Whittaker says anything in the morning."

"Where do they run?" Arnold continued. "The mines - where do they run?"

"They run for miles and miles underneath the town," his dad replied, clearly very concerned about what Arnold had told him. His parents left the room and Arnold sat and finished his tea. He knew that his dad wasn't telling him everything he knew about the coal mines but one way or another he intended to find out. Once he was done eating, he headed up to his bedroom and attempted some of his homework. Arnold felt as though all his spare time was spent either dealing with school or training and that he couldn't catch a break at the moment.

After pushing himself so hard at training, he felt as though he had little energy left to work out the various maths equations that he needed to do by the morning. Arnold hated algebra more than any other subject at school. He found it a pointless exercise as who on earth used algebra these days or ever for that matter. Arnold scribbled down a few answers before eventually losing his patience with it and putting his pencil down. Looking down at his desk, he felt that he could just put his head down and go to sleep; he felt well and truly drained. Trying to juggle school and training was catching up with him and he was only three weeks into the new school year.

There was a knock at the door and his dad pushed the door open slightly.

"Come in." He walked through and sat at the end of Arnold's bed. He looked very serious.

"Something doesn't seem right at the Chichen. Mr. Whittaker meeting up with Mayor Redburn when no one is around? That is strange in itself but considering re-opening the coal mine? There's no money in it so what else are they planning?"

"What are you going to do?" asked Arnold.

"Sit tight. We need to just observe for now. Think you can do that, son?" Arnold nodded. It felt strange to be doing something like this around the Chichen, but with his dad onside, it didn't feel so wrong. He was curious to find out what was going on. He also wanted to know what Mr. Redburn would want with the coal mine if it didn't have anything to do with money.

Arnold wasn't the biggest fan of Mr. Whittaker, but he was the Elder of that region and as such was very much respected. So, such a strange and potentially dangerous idea like gaining access to the mines just didn't make any sense, to Arnold or his dad. Something very odd was afoot and Arnold intended to find out what on earth was going on.

CHAPTER 13

Bang!

He clattered into the side of the wooden hut with considerable force, instantly knocking him sick. His head felt fuzzy from the blow, but he refused to stay on the floor. He refused to show any weakness.

He had been through this process many times as the woman continuously beat him though he didn't know why. It had been like this for a few years now. For long periods, he found himself left to fend for himself. He had even taught himself to grow vegetables throughout the year. He had managed to bring back tins of food from time to time when he found himself in the other world, but he still didn't have any control over where or even when he ended up. He especially liked the tinned peaches in syrup and bacon grill that he had managed to get his hands on. He was a survivalist even though he was only fifteen years old. He had needed to learn. Otherwise, he simply wouldn't be alive.

She would arrive, sporadically, out of the blue and when least expected. All she would do is turn up, inflict pain and suffering on him, tell him how disappointed she was in him and then leave. This was a process he had gone through time and time again for as long back as he could remember. Sometimes it would take a few days to recover from his injuries, sometimes weeks. The horrific scar he had on his face had taken months to heal fully. Even though it was from when he was a boy, it still burned every day as though a red-hot poker was pressed continuously against his face. It was a sensation that he had become accustomed to, one that he had to accept and learn to get on with, just like these intermittent beatings.

He hated her with every ounce of his being, but he never tried to run or tried to fight back. It just made things worse and the beatings more severe. His legs were buckling and he recognised the familiar feeling of being winded. The woman grabbed him by the scruff of his already tattered clothes and lifted him towards her as if he weighed nothing. Her strength was unbelievable and something he aspired to have.

"You are pathetic," she growled, her anger towards him intense and confusing. His gaze did not move from hers as he tried to show that he was stronger, that he was not afraid. This didn't stop her. She slapped him across the face, throwing him to the ground. He bounced off the floor and ground to a slow stop against the gravel.

"Come on. You have had long enough. Show me! " she sneered, appearing more impatient at his abhorrent uselessness. There was only one reason she had allowed him to live this long and that was because she had one use for him, an ability he had shown many years ago but clearly still didn't have control over. That's what all these beatings were for, to try and trigger a reaction from him. Despite her best efforts, it had never worked. She had nurtured him at an early age, not out of want but out of need. His very flesh and blood were what she needed to escape this place. It was becoming apparent that she was going to have to wait longer given that at fifteen he was unable to summon a spirit beast. The longer this went on, the more likely that he was a menial. Where would he draw that power to drift across to the other side? Because one way or another, she was going to get back to the real world.

He attempted to climb to his feet once more, but he felt

his body pinned to the floor. He realised that the dragon had slammed its large foot into him, grinding him into the ground. He hadn't felt this power or force for many years. She must be furious for her spirit beast to have shown itself.

He grinned to himself, ensuring that he did not show this on his face; he had been waiting for this moment. Taking beating after beating for all these years purposely so that from time to time, he would be confronted with this magnificent spirit beast. His opportunity now was to study it intently, how it moved, how it breathed, how it reacted to the surroundings. She had played into his hands and lost her temper, more so than usual anyway. The one thing that he was certain of was that he wanted a dragon spirit for himself, something that he would achieve no matter what.

When she finally left, he was a bloodied mess on the ground; drained of energy and exhausted. He had put everything he had in to not passing out as he was tossed about like a rag doll by the spirit beast. He would close his eyes and count to ten in an attempt to distract himself. It rarely worked; he felt everything; every blow, every claw mark that was etched into his back over the years. He lay there, staring up at the clear blue sky above him, turning his head to discharge the blood in his mouth. The sun shone brightly. His eyes looked as though they were squinting, but it was due to swelling, having received numerous blows to his face. This was one of the worst beatings he had received. He thought he must have been knocked unconscious because the last thing he remembered was that he had his eyes tightly shut and was counting slowly in his head to counteract the clawing, burning sensation down his back. The pain had been unbearable. When he had finally come round, she and her spirit beast had gone. He lay on his back in the worst pain he had ever experienced. A manic smile erupted and he began to laugh to himself. The beating was worth every ounce of pain that he was now feeling.

He reached down and pulled his ripped t-shirt up slightly. It was still there, tucked into the front of his pants.

He had managed to grab it without her noticing when she had scooped him up in the air, like a seasoned pickpocket. He pulled the item out and lifted it above him to look at it. It was the dagger that she had always carried with her. One that he was sure was an artefact and had a unique ability. All he had to do now was figure out how to use it and he needed to figure that out quickly knowing that as soon as she found out that the blade was missing, she would be back.

Staring intently at the decorated hilt, he knew that the base was made from ebony and that the blade from ivory. The darkness of the hilt was as black as the night itself. When he was younger, he had seen her studying the blade intently and chanting various incantations, but up until now, she had been unable to use it. She had remained unsuccessful all these years in getting it to work.

Knowing what may happen should she return, he closed his eyes once more and began to count to try and get through the immense pain he was feeling. His back felt like it was on fire and he knew that he couldn't take another beating, not one more blow. At this point, a tremendous wave of sadness came over him. What had he done to deserve this life? He had been an innocent baby when he had been born in this world alone with no one looking out for him other than that evil woman. How he hated her for what she had done to him throughout his life. Feeling a knot in his stomach, he felt as though he couldn't swallow, as though he had eaten glass. It was at this point that he released an emotion he had not shown since he was a little boy and tears began to stream down his face. They left streaks of clean skin where they had removed the dirt from his face. His feelings of sorrow made him wonder if it would ever end and he contemplated using the knife in his hands to finish it all.

Then he noticed something through his stinging eyes. The blade was emitting an orange glow. He could feel its warmth and it felt as though the unbearable misery he was feeling started to lift, leaving him calmer. He stared at the blade intently mesmerised by its illuminated beauty.

The feeling intensified, he felt his grip tighten around the blade as though he couldn't let go. He sat upright and began to get to his feet, something that just five minutes before he did not feel strong enough to do. The glow around the blade became bigger and began to draw up his arms engulfing his entire body like flames. More flames danced around him, making him feel as though he was wrapped in a warm blanket. This was the warm embrace that he had craved his entire life and the pain he was feeling began to subside. It was like the blade was listening to him and soothing his internal and external pain.

He continued to emit a bright orange glow until he felt something connect with him inside. It was a feeling that he couldn't quite recognise, but for the first time in his entire life, he didn't feel alone. From within his body, something escaped. Through the light, a large lion stepped outwards from his body, followed by a second one. They stood in front of him, both equally powerful and majestic. Each had a different look, however.

Finding himself warped into a zoo a few years ago, he had seen lions. The two in front of him did not have the same appearance. Neither of them had a mane around their sizable heads. The one on the left was slightly smaller than the other and carried a massive scar on one of its cheeks. It stood in front of him and he gasped. They were so intimidating to look at from so close. One released a loud growl which made his heart flicker; the magnificent beast began to walk towards him slowly until it stood in his personal space.

The creature then bowed its head to him and reaching forward, he placed his open hand on its head slowly. Suddenly, the connection he had felt before intensified and he could feel the lion's feelings and thoughts as if they were his own. It was the strangest sensation and one that he immediately embraced. Within moments he felt strong and powerful, but he wasn't stupid; he knew he would not be powerful enough to take her and her dragon spirit beast on. At least now he finally stood a chance. He now finally had a spirit beast to call his own. Two of them in fact. He looked at the two giant lions and was mesmerised by their beauty and their strength. They both sat there calmly looking at him as their tails flipped and slapped the floor sporadically, the larger one of the two let out a giant yawn.

He felt another strange sensation, one that he had not felt for some time and he knew what was coming. Next to him, the air became distorted and the frosted portal opened. A force of energy blew out around it with more power than usual. He felt a pull towards it; it was magnetic and he had no control over it. He began to slide towards the portal, it was drawing him in before eventually, he fell forwards inside. He felt instantly disorientated before a feeling of weightlessness came over him and the sensation of falling surprised him. He had come through in mid-air at the top of a steep hill. He fell around eight feet and landed on the wrong side of the hill and began bouncing down violently, feeling every rock, shrub and tree that he collided with on his way to the bottom. He lay on the floor staring up into the sky; his body was aching and throbbing from head to toe. He wondered what he must have done to deserve this. His happiness at suddenly having two magnificent spirit beasts to call his own had been short-lived. He didn't know where he was and he had no idea how long he would be here.

CHAPTER 14

It was a Saturday and Arnold took refuge in the fact that, at least for the next two days, he didn't need to go to school. He did know that he would have to go to the Chichen at some point to carry on practising spirit wielding in a safe environment. He still hadn't had any success, but Arnold was even more determined to succeed. However, he was still no nearer to finding out anything more about the mysterious creature that had attacked him at the Bramley lock up.

He had his plan for the day which was to spend some time at the lockup with Everett, George and Marrok. Arnold wanted to go through some of his grandad's old books to see if they could find anything out about the spirit beast that had attacked him. Arnold was already at the lockup and searching for a specific book he had thought he had seen when they first found his grandad's belongings. He had just finished rummaging through some old boxes when the door to the lockup began to slide back.

"Hey." Marrok walked into the room. "Just you here?"

"Everett and George are on their way." Marrok came to stand next to Arnold.

"What are you doing?" Arnold picked up one box and placed it on top of another to create a bit more space for the four of them. "I'm looking for some old books. I saw one that looked like a scrapbook with drawings of different spirit beasts. I want to find it."

"I can help, what did it look like?" Marrok offered, looking around.

"It was an old leather book with a stone in the centre of the cover, like a pale blue colour."

"Random, it can't be that hard to find." The two of them continued rummaging around looking for it for a short while, rustling through different boxes and cabinets.

"You know you really should take more care of the things in here boys." They both turned round to see Everett and George stood at the entrance to the lockup. Arnold thought Everett was looking particularly pretty today; she was wearing some dark jeans and a white vest top. George had a fifties style dress on with little red roses all over it along with her boots and her beany hat.

"Arnold wants to find a book, leather thing with a bluish stone in the centre of it."

"Oh, I think it's over here," George said, walking over to a cupboard and pulling out a drawer to reveal the book they were looking for.

"Brill!" Arnold walked across and took the book from her and began to flick through it.

"Something particular you're looking for?" George asked.

"I think it's my grandad's old journal from back when he was a Doyen." On each page of the journal, Arnold found different sketches of spirit beasts and a small explanation on the opposite side to describe each spirit beast's traits. The first page had an outline of an Elk which had been his grandad's spirit beast. The next page had a giraffe, then a hippo followed by an owl. Everett peered from over Arnold's shoulder to catch a look at what he was looking at.

"Wow, your grandad was good at drawing."

"He was, wasn't he. This has got loads of information in it." On the page with the hippo, he noticed that he had scribbled Charles Grey down at the top of the page. "Looks like he has written down some of the names of people that have these spirit beasts." He turned the page. There was a detailed sketch of a dragon; the detail within the drawing was such that Arnold instantly recognised this spirit beast as the one that had chased him in the spirit world. Its razor-sharp teeth matched by its pointed scales that stuck out at the bottom of its wings. At the top of the page, he saw the name Helen Ethon, confirming to him that this was, in fact, his grandma's spirit beast.

He continued to turn the pages until one made him stop, catching his attention instantly as he recognised the spirit beast he could see. It had sharp fangs and pointed ears and a mouth that protruded from its face like a cat or a dog, but definitely more feline. Then he looked at the patterning of the spirit beast and could see it had rounded dots all over it with a darker outer edge. The spirit beast resembled what he had come face to face with outside of the lockup. This spirit beast looked more humanoid in form than any Arnold had ever seen and this is what had been puzzling him. As with the other pages opposite the sketch, there was a handwritten entry.

"Have you found anything?" Marrok asked.

"Night Sun?" Arnold spoke as he read the words at the top of the page.

"What do you mean?" George looked just as puzzled as everyone else in the room.

"That's what it's called, the creature that attacked me. It's called Night Sun."

"I've never heard of a spirit beast that goes by that name," Everett said. "That sounds more like a name than an animal. What else does it say?" Arnold started to read the page out loud to the others.

"Worshipped by the Almec, Night Sun is seen as the reincarnation of an ancient deity. The Were-Jaguar."

"Were-Jaguar?" George repeated loudly.

At this point, it clicked into place; why the creature had felt so familiar, particularly those eyes. How could he have been so stupid and not realised this sooner? The marking's matched that of a jaguar, he had the information all along and just not realised.

"It's Otto! The thing that attacked me – it's Otto!"

"What? That can't be right. How is that even possible?" Everett was in a state of absolute disbelief at what Arnold was saying to them. "Why would he? How is he?" The questions were coming out of her mouth faster than Arnold was thinking of them himself.

Arnold was stunned. How had this happened to his best friend? He had a jaguar spirit beast but what had happened for him to turn into that ferocious creature. The wildness in its eyes was something that had stuck with Arnold long after their last confrontation.

"I don't know how but it's him. I know it is." Arnold was sure of it and spoke with conviction. There was a noise outside, like scuffled footsteps in the dirt.

"Damn it," the voice from outside cursed. Marrok shot to the front of the lockup to see who it was outside.

"Otto?" Arnold moved to the entrance to see Otto sat on his backside as if he had just fallen over.

"It's you, how could you?"

"It wasn't me, Arnold. I promise." His voice was panicked "It was me, but not me if that makes sense?" he continued to stutter. Arnold didn't know what to think or feel. He didn't know if he was angry at being attacked by his best friend or upset that he hadn't told him what was happening to him.

"You're Night Sun," Arnold said, his voice raised.

"Night what?" Otto got back to his feet and dusted himself down.

"Why are you here?" Everett interrogated.

"Want to go another round is that it?" George followed up.

"Wait, no, why would I?" Otto was on the defensive and did not appear to understand what he was being accused of. "I don't understand what is happening to me…what has happened to me." Tears filled his eyes. He looked desperate for help. He also looked frightened, something that Arnold had never seen in him before.

"You attacked me!" Arnold explained.

"And me!" George added.

"It wasn't you though, was it? Otto, you changed into something. It was your jaguar spirit beast, but you had turned into it." Arnold's initial anger had turned into compassion for Otto, seeing him stood there looking so vulnerable.

"It first happened about a week after the Chichen threw me out. I had no one to go to Arnold. My dad took me away to see my family. They see it as a possession and tried to do things to remove my spirit beast from me. Horrible things, all summer." His eyes began to well once more and Otto looked as though he was ready to burst into tears. "It's the dagger. It did something to us. I can't control it; it just happens."

"Where's the dagger now? I can ask the Chichen."

"No," Marrok interjected, "If you go to the Chichen, they will take Otto away."

"I'm not a lab rat. I don't want to lose my spirit beast. I don't want to be a menial," Otto pleaded.

"We need to help him, Arnold." Everett walked across and threw her arms around Otto and gave him a huge hug. Otto began to sob into her arms and put his arms around her to hug her back. Arnold walked across and wrapped his arms around the two of them, followed by George.

"We are here for you, Otto, whatever we can do." Arnold had his friend's back. He was in a bad way, but he needed their help to figure out what to do.

"Where is the dagger? We could ask your granny, George." Arnold knew that she had the knowledge given that she was a shaman and might have more information for them.

"I don't know. My dad said he'd put it somewhere safe?" Otto's response defensive.

"Right if we head to Granny's shop we can go see if she can help us." George directed.

Arnold walked to the front of the lockup and placed his hand on the side, triggering the locking system and securing the container. He turned to face Otto.

"Come on, let's go. You're going to be ok, mate."

It wasn't long before the five of them had made the short journey across town and found themselves at the shop. The town was quite busy today as it was a Saturday and everyone was taking the opportunity to get their shopping done. Car after car was passing on the main street with people coming in and out of the different shops. The quietest shop on the road was the very one that was their destination. Technology had changed and people were happy to take tablets to cure different ailments rather than take herbal remedies. Not that many people went to see traditional healers to help them with pain relief anymore. This surprised Arnold given how much the remedy he had been given had helped him.

They opened the door to the shop and the old bell above them rang to signify their arrival. They waited at the front of the shop for George's granny to come out from the back. She didn't appear.

"Granny?" George called out. No one responded and the shop was eerily quiet.

"Maybe she can't hear us," Everett pointed out. George lifted the folding part of the counter over and walked through. The door to the back had a multi-coloured beaded door blinds preventing anyone from looking through. George pulled them to one side; the beads made a unique noise as they all the beads clattered into one another.

"GRANNY!" George cried as she shot through the doorway and into the back. Arnold quickly followed, he could see George's granny laid out on the floor. Her skin was pale, almost colourless. George was knelt to the side of her, leaning into her and sobbing hysterically. Arnold walked over and placed his hand on her granny's wrist; her skin was cold to touch. There was nothing they could do for her and so he knelt next to George and wrapped his arms around her. Everett and the others came to the doorway and were shocked at what they could see. Arnold turned to face them.

"Someone call an ambulance and the Chichen," he requested. "George's granny is dead."

CHAPTER 15

Arnold stood at the side of the coffin along with the rest of his friends as they paid their final respects to George's granny. The ceremony had been beautiful, with George reading a poem she had written for her during her eulogy. George stood on the opposite side of them with her dads on either side of her. She was wearing a black lace dress and she looked distraught. Her granny was her best friend who she spent most of her spare time with and now George would never get to see her again. Arnold understood how she felt, but he had not had a chance to speak with her following her death as she had spent the last four days at home with her family and her phone off. Knowing George as they did, they had all respected her wishes and kept their distance. She would not want people's sympathy and would just want to grieve with her parents.

The coroners' report had said that she had had a heart attack but with everything that had been going on Arnold had initially questioned whether it was due to something more sinister. However, he was relieved to find out that it was natural causes. She was an elderly lady in her eighties after all. The timing couldn't have been any worse with her being the only shaman in the town and the only person they could think of to go to with their Otto problem. Now she was gone and they were all back to square one.

The coffin was lowered slowly into the ground and George leaned into her dad, her crying intensified. Her other dad then hugged the two of them together to comfort them both. They were such a close family and it was hard for Arnold to see the pain they were all going through. George and her parents stepped forward and threw soil onto the coffin and headed back to the cars together, George's head tucked firmly into her dad's side.

"I hope she's ok," Arnold said to the others.

"She will be. She appreciates us all being here," Everett said. "I will call round in the morning to see her."

Her family had chosen to have the wake at the house with only immediate family and the school had allowed them to attend the funeral but requested that they go back to school in the afternoon.

"We'd best head back to school," Everett sighed. Arnold looked across to where the cars were parked and could see what looked like the mayor's car. Focusing, his sight was zooming in on the car and he could see Mayor Redburn sat in the back of the car looking out at them with Mr. Whittaker sat next to him.

"Why would your dad be here, Otto?" he asked.

"Huh?" Otto grunted in response.

"He's down there in his car with Mr. Whittaker," Arnold continued.

"I don't know. Strange that - my dad hates Mr. Whittaker for throwing me out of the Chichen." Everyone else had left the funeral and were getting into their cars to leave. The four of them had decided to head across the field opposite as it took them back towards the school. They were part way across the field when Otto suddenly stopped and bent over holding his stomach.

"You ok?" Arnold asked.

Otto didn't respond. He had his eyes closed and began to breathe heavily. "It...it's happening!" He dropped to his knees in agony.

"What's happening?" Marrok asked.

"You all need to leave now!" Otto hissed through the pain. Arnold realised what was happening. "We can help you."

"I don't want to hurt anyone. I can't control this. You all need to get away from me!" His breathing was heavy; Otto was trying to breathe through the pain he was experiencing and was clearly in agony. His body started to contort violently which he had no control over. "Go!" he growled at them. "Wh- why are you stiiillll heeeeere?!" He was struggling to talk, the pain was clearly unbearable.

"We want to help you!" Arnold hated seeing Otto in all this pain and reached out to comfort him. Otto's bones began to make a cracking noise like large tree branches snapping. His bones were breaking and Otto began to scream at the process. He looked up; his eyes appeared different, like the Otto they knew was disappearing. His face had started to change shape and the jaguar markings began to take form on his skin. He reached forward and grabbed hold of the ground in front of him. They could all see his hands changing shape and large claws began to protrude from his fingertips.

Otto then stood taller than all of them. His body had completely changed; he had become his spirit beast. He had become Night Sun the were-jaguar. He let out a ferocious roar towards the group, but none of them moved.

"It's ok. We are here." Arnold put his hands up to be as unhostile as he could be. He stepped forward towards Otto slowly. Otto let out another roar, his breathing was heavy and produced a growling noise. Arnold continued to walk towards him slowly to show he wasn't frightened and that he wanted to help him. He got too close and received a full force backhand knocking him back to the ground. Everett and Marrok quickly helped him up.

"Arnold, what do we do?" Marrok asked. "Someone is going to get hurt."

"We need to stop him." Everett stepped forward and began to emit a soft purple glow. Her boar appeared before her; it had grown in size and now had larger, protruding tusks coming from its mouth, its large body showing that it had increased in power. Arnold then began to concentrate. His light blue auro engulfed his body before his eagle spirit beast flew out from within him and landed on the ground in front of him, its large wingspan spread out in a show of its power. He looked across at Marrok, unsure whether or not he had a spirit beast. He had never asked him. Marrok nodded and began to focus. An orange glow began to generate through his auro. Moments later, a white wolf ran from inside him and stood on all fours next to the eagle and the boar. It had a thick mane of hair with red eyes that contrasted against the beast's ice white colour. It let out a shrill howl as it fixed its gaze upon Otto, bearing its teeth.

"A wolf, that's awesome." Arnold brain fixed on what traits Marrok must have for a wolf spirit beast but quickly snapped out of those thoughts and focus on Otto.

"Thanks," Marrok replied without shifting his eyes. Otto stood, growling in his spirit form. He was behaving erratically and looked as though it wasn't able to focus on them. Saliva dripping from his open mouth and his razor-sharp teeth on full display, his stare was switching between the three spirit beasts that stood before him.

"What do we do now?" Marrok asked, seeking direction from Arnold.

"We can't let him get away, no matter what!" Arnold commanded.

Otto ran towards them at speed and the boar and the wolf set off running at him equally as fast. Arnold's eagle took flight and flew in the same direction as the others. The boar reached him first, but Otto hurdled over the top of it, dragging its claws down its back in the process. Everett winced and the boar made a shrieking noise. Using his momentum, Otto vaulted the boar and hurled itself head-on into the wolf who let out a yelp as the two of them grappled with each other on the floor. Otto, however, was much stronger and bit down on the wolf's neck causing it to let out a further yelp. Arnold's eagle swooped in, but Otto was quick to assess its pattern of movement and jumped out of the way. The boar came charging from the side and crashed into the beast, breaking its firm bite on the wolf and knocking it backwards. It let out a growl and launched itself at the boar, grabbing it with both of its hands and embedding its claws into its sides. Using its momentum, it lifted the boar into the air and slammed it down to the ground. Everett dropped to her knees having felt the pain her boar was experiencing.

"He's too strong!" she cried. The eagle swooped down at Otto again and grabbed it with its dagger-like talons on his shoulders to lift him in the air. Otto reached up and grabbed hold of it, slamming it straight onto the ground below him. Arnold held his side, but his pain threshold was higher than the others.

Otto continued his run towards the group and Arnold stepped in front of Everett and Marrok bracing himself for impact. A moment later he realised that the impact hadn't happened; Otto had run past them and was charging across the field.

"What is going on?" Everett shouted.

"We can't let him run through town in that form, someone will get hurt and he is going to be captured." Marrok set off running after the out of control spirit beast. "Come on!"

Arnold immediately followed even though they didn't have a plan for what to do once they caught up with him. Otto was faster than the three of them, but they were still quick and they covered the ground at speed, managing to keep Otto in their sights. They couldn't catch up in time and it was only going to be a few moments before he reached the main street that led into town. Arnold's eagle flew overhead following Otto into town, swooping down and clattering into the back of him, knocking him over. Marrok's white wolf overtook them and threw itself into Otto's side, delaying him from climbing back to his feet.

"Otto!" Arnold called, trying to get his attention, "You need to stop!" Otto continued to grapple with the eagle and wolf and did not respond to Arnold's calls. "Listen to me! listen to my voice!" Arnold shouted, trying to get through to him. Otto began to rain down blows on Marrok's spirit beast, his wildness taking over him. "Otto stop!" Arnold cried, "you're going to kill him!" Marrok had fallen to the floor, unable to cope with the pain he was sharing with his spirit beast. His connection was strong, but he didn't appear experienced.

Arnold ran across and grabbed hold of the back of Otto and tried pulling him, a flailing elbow was the reward he got for this, but he managed to block it. "Come on, listen to me." His persistence appeared to pay off as Otto seemed to respond to him momentarily. Arnold could tell this through his eyes as they looked different, softer like they did before Otto had transformed. There was sadness in them; sorrow solidifying to Arnold that his best friend was not in control of what he was doing. "Come on, Otto. I know you are in there," he said, trying to use a more calming tone.

Otto stopped and stood still, his erratic movements slowing and an air of control coming over him. He moved away from the wolf which lay injured on the floor and walked slowly towards Arnold.

Arnold's eagle moved next to the wolf and wrapped its wings around him, creating a half-dome shield around it while also using its energy to help it recover from its wounds. Otto continued his steady walk to Arnold.

"Can you hear me?" Arnold asked. The beast nodded. "Can you understand me?" The beast nodded again. Arnold couldn't believe it; Otto had regained control.

This was short-lived, however and Otto began to stagger and shake his head, his movements becoming once more erratic. He shook his head and started to grunt and growl before turning away from Arnold and setting off running once more. The beast dropped onto all fours and his speed increased dramatically. They had failed and Otto was about to hit the main street where everyone would be able to see him. On its way towards the eagle, which was still wrapped around the wolf, Otto crashed into it head-on, knocking it to the side. Both the eagle and wolf lay on the floor, injured from the encounter. Otto continued his run onto the main street.

"Stay with your Wolf!" Arnold told Marrok as he set off running after Otto, despite him being so far back. He needed to catch up to him and stop him, but this was difficult given that he had no idea where Otto was going or what he was doing.

Arnold kept him in sight using his enhanced vision, but the truth was unless Otto stopped, he was not going to catch up with him. Keeping his eyes on him, he saw Otto hit the street and straight away he heard the screams begin to ring out. Arnold reached the street with Otto still way ahead as he ran down the main road, people screaming as he hurdled over car after car as they came at him the opposite way, a loud metallic scratching noise leaving claw marks where he had touched the vehicles. Arnold knew it was only a matter of time before the Doyens arrived and he could feel his stomach churning with what might happen when they did. His throat was dry through the overexertion and his head was pounding from the adrenaline that was coursing through him.

Otto suddenly stopped in the middle of the road and began staring directly at one of the shops. It was George's granny's remedy store. After a short moment, he jumped through the window, the glass shattering everywhere. Seizing his opportunity, Arnold put every ounce of his energy into catching up and he was outside the store before he knew it. A crowd of people began running away from the vicinity of the shop and Arnold could see people on their phones, most likely calling the Chichen. Arnold ran and hurdled through the broken window, the glass crunching below his feet as he ground it into the floor when he landed. Arnold could hear Otto in the back of the store, crashing around. Arnold was puzzled as to why he would be in this store. He had seemed to specifically target this store as if he was looking for something in particular.

"Otto!" He called. The grunts stopped and Arnold could hear a growl start to call back to him from the backroom aggressively.

"I just want to help you."

"You need...get away...no control." The voice sounded different than usual, deeper, huskier than how he usually spoke but it was Otto. This threw Arnold, but it solidified his thoughts more than ever that Otto needed his help.

"What are you doing?" he asked, still confused as to why Otto had chosen to come here.

"I feel the pull...like magnet...no control," Otto's faltering voice called back to Arnold. He heard the back door to the rear of the building open and was sure there was more than one pair of footsteps. Arnold stepped forward towards the back to see what was happening when he heard the call from behind him.

"Whoever is in there, you need to come out!" Arnold froze. The voice he heard belonged to his dad. "This is the Chichen."

Arnold could no longer hear Otto behind him and he presumed he had exited the building. He decided to exit out of the rear of the building to try and trail him again.

"I'm coming in," Arthur announced. Arnold stepped back towards the door and made it into the back room as his dad entered the shop from the front, his footsteps slowly crunching the glass underneath him. Arnold moved quietly to the back door, partly opening it so he could exit. "Don't move!" Arthur bellowed once more.

Otto ran before Arnold reached him and vaulted the wall at the back of the yard before escaping down the alleyway. He heard his dad's footsteps speeding up as he gave chase after Otto. Arnold knew he needed to protect him from the

Chichen. He was running as fast as he could to reach the bottom of the alley, navigating the uneven cobbled floor beneath him. Arnold knew he wasn't going to outrun his dad but needed to keep him distracted so that Otto could get away. Arnold could hear fierce growling ahead and Otto stepped out from the bottom of the alley in front of him. His height and frame were physically imposing. His clothes were heavily ripped, displaying the intricate pattern of a jaguar that was now all over his fur-covered body. He was baring his teeth and saliva was pouring from his face as he began to growl wildly.

Otto vaulted past him and headed towards Arthur at pace on all fours once more. Arnold heard the roar from his dad's bear as he summoned it and it began running at speed towards the were-jaguar. The two came together, lifting their front paws as the two of them slammed into each other. Razor-sharp, jagged teeth began gnawing at each other. The powerful grizzly knocked Otto into the wall using its large head, the wall cracking with the impact. Arnold ran back towards the fighting wanting to stop his dad and Otto from hurting one another.

"Dad, no!"

"Arnold?" Arthur looked puzzled "What are you-?" Arnold's path was blocked by the two of them, as they continued to bounce each other from one side of the alley to the other.

"Stop, dad!" he cried, "You need to stop!"

The grizzly bear snapped its jaws around Otto's side, who let out a roar in anger. The grizzly tightened its grip and flung Otto sideways, skimming over the floor before crashing into the wall on the opposite side. The grizzly stood up on its hind legs, its intimidating size standing at around seven feet tall. It let out a roar that shook Arnold to the core. Arnold threw himself forwards in between Otto and the bear "Stop!" His arms were outstretched as he tried to make himself as big as possible. "You're going to hurt him!"

"Get out of the way, Arnold, what are you doing?"

"You can't!"

"We need to bring it in, whatever the hell that thing is," Arthur shouted. Arnold stared at his dad; he had no intention of moving as he didn't want either of them to get hurt.

"You need to trust me, dad. He doesn't know what he is doing." Arthur frowned.

"Who?"

Otto jumped up from the floor and let out an ear-deafening roar with Arnold standing no further than a foot away. He could feel the heat from his breath on his face. The slimy drool from his mouth splattered across his face. Arnold was shaking. He didn't want to move out the way and slammed his hands against Otto's chest and put all his weight into pushing him back against the wall.

"You need to stop!" He looked up at Otto. "Look at me." Otto cast his gaze down on him. He was so much taller than he usually was and his eyes still looked wild. He began to push against Arnold's hands, the force causing Arnold to slide backwards. "Please, Otto." Otto shook his head and his eyes became recognisable once more. "Focus on my voice," Arnold said calmly. Otto appeared to understand and stood still for a moment, more human-like than before. His breathing became laboured as he stopped pushing against Arnold. The grizzly bear dropped back to all fours, a slow grumble emitting from under its closed mouth.

Otto looked at Arnold with great sadness as his bones slowly began to crack back into shape. Slowly he began to change back into human form, the jaguar markings all over his body changing back to normal skin. Dropping to his knees, exhausted from the transformation, Otto slumped back against the wall.

"Otto?" Arthur called before his spirit beast began to dissipate back inside him. He ran across to the two of them. Arnold was kneeling next to Otto to check on him. He was weary and looked ready to pass out.

"How? You were -?" Arthur seemed unable to process what he had just seen. "You're a -"

"Were-jaguar," Otto mumbled as he attempted to get back to his feet.

"I'm going to have to take you in, Otto."

"You can't, dad!" Arnold protested.

"The whole town has seen him, Arnold. If I don't, then they are going to send more people from the other Chichens to find him."

"They will kill him," Arnold pleaded. Otto looked scared; it was slowly dawning on him what had just happened to him.

"I didn't have any control over myself."

"Even more reason for me to bring you in, Otto. It's not safe." Otto began to shake.

"Please, Mr. Ethon, I'm scared." Arnold stood between Otto and his dad.

"We need to help him, dad. If we take him to the Chichen, who knows what they will do to him." A siren could be heard at the other side of the building, its noise echoing down the alleyway.

"That will be Mr. Whittaker."

"Dad, you need to help him. Please! Just until we try and figure something out." Arthur looked at the back of the shop before looking at the two of them.

"Go," he said, looking unsure of his decision. Arnold breathed a sigh of relief and hooked Otto's arm around his neck and the two of them began to make their way down the alleyway and out of sight. Away from danger and away from the Chichen.

CHAPTER 16

"What does it feel like?" Arnold and Otto had made it back to his house. Arnold was sat on his beanbag with Otto sprawled out on his bed, still recovering from his transformation into the were-jaguar.

"It hurts like hell. The pain is like nothing else. I feel my bones breaking as I am transforming. Then it goes dark and all I can feel is an empty loneliness." Otto breathed out a huge sigh as he flaked on the bed. "What do we do now?" Arnold shrugged.

"I don't know. I'm hoping my dad will know what to do." Arnold heard the front door open and then slam and footsteps straight upstairs before his dad walked straight into his room.

"What on earth. How are you? Are either of you hurt?"

"All I know, Mr. Ethon, is that when Sue stabbed my spirit beast with her dagger, something happened to me when I tried to pull it out of him. That's when all this started."

"Why didn't you come to us at the Chichen?"

"Because I was thrown out, disgraced for my actions. Sue was going to take my jaguar and there was no other way of stopping her. I went to my dad, he told me to keep quiet and took me to spend the summer with my family to try more traditional ways of healing me."

"That worked, then," Arnold said, feeling annoyed. If Otto had to come to them, they could have helped him sooner.

"I was told to distance myself from everyone when we came back. My great uncle had said that I had become fused with my spirit beast. When I touched that dagger, I reabsorbed him but in an unnatural way."

"Like a form of corruption? This is not good, Otto," Arthur added, looking as concerned as ever.

"My great uncle said that it has happened before but a very long time ago. My dad has reached out to a group of people called the Almec."

"The Almec? Otto you do not want to get into bed with those fanatics," Arthur warned. Arnold remembered that the Almec was mentioned in his grandad's journal.

"They worship the were-jaguar as a deity. Night-Sun," he blurted out.

"How do you know that?" His dad asked.

"I read it."

"Read it where?" Arnold was beginning to feel an interrogation coming on.

Arnold didn't want to tell the truth, so instead, he decided to answer with a question.

"Why?"

"Because the Chichen keeps any texts about the Almec. They are kept at the grand temple for a reason. Somewhere that you do not have access to." This confused Arnold. Why would his grandad have had the information that he did in his journal but kept it from the Chichen when he was a Doyen and then an Elder?

"You know what, we have bigger things to deal with. What were you doing at that shop?" His dad switched the target of his interrogation. Otto shrugged.

"I honestly don't know. When I transform, I'm not in control. It's like I'm a passenger; there are times when I can breakthrough, but it isn't me."

"So, you have no control, or someone else is controlling you," Arthur pressed.

"Like a spirit beast?" Arnold concluded.

"You mean I'm now a spirit beast?" Otto looked dejected at this information.

"You're corrupted. If I had to make a suggestion, it would be that whoever has that dagger is the person who is controlling you."

"Your dad? You said your dad had the dagger." Arnold was sure of it but then why would Mayor Redburn control Otto and make him transform before breaking into George's granny's shop? It just did not make any sense. "He was there, wasn't he? You gave him something at the back door?"

"Then he made you attack me." Arthur was less than impressed that Mayor Redburn had wanted Otto to attack him.

"I'm so sorry." Otto cut a sad figure. He looked tired and weary from everything that he had been through. He did, however, look better for being able to share his secret with someone.

"Don't be. This wasn't you," Arthur reassured Otto, but he did not answer.

"He's trying to help me," Otto explained, "He told me there might be a way to separate us. He just needs somewhere with a high connection to the spirit world."

"Why not use the tower?" Arnold asked.

"Because it's not powerful enough."

"The coal mine?" Arthur muttered, the realization dawning on him. "He wants to use the deepest part of the coal mine which is right in the centre of town. The energy levels there are astronomical, it's the real reason why it was shut down." Suddenly, it all began to make sense to Arnold. Mayor Redburn wished to secretly open the mine so that he could try and separate Otto from his spirit beast. The main question now was how was he going to do it.

"Do you remember what you gave him at the shop?"

"No." Otto looked utterly dejected.

"It's most likely linked to what your dad has planned. I mean, it must be but why the remedy shop?" Arthur said, thinking out loud. The Chichen was involved at some level. Mr. Whittaker and Mayor Redburn had been meeting up and discussing the opening of the coal mines. Did Mr. Whittaker know the real reason for Mayor Redburn wanting to open it?

Arnold didn't know what the best move was to make now. They could either go to the Chichen and take the risk that they would not then lock Otto up for "his safety" or go to Mayor Redburn to try and see what his plan was in its entirety. The problem with the latter idea was that Mayor Redburn was incredibly hostile towards Arnold the last time he saw him, for the part he perceived him to have played in Otto being thrown out of the Chichen. He wasn't going to want to talk to Arnold and deep down, Arnold was fully aware of what the Chichen would most likely do to Otto, so he didn't want to go down that path, either.

"What do we do, dad?" he asked, hoping he had some better ideas.

"I don't know, son. For now, I think we need to sit tight. People have seen Otto and the Chichen are now looking for him. Otto, you need to ensure that if you are to transform again, you will not be seen for your safety and others. At least until we have a plan. I can't know where you are Otto, if this were to happen again, I would have no choice but to take you in."

"I understand, Mr. Ethon. Thank you." Arnold felt proud of his dad for helping Otto, but he also knew what position this placed both of them in with the Chichen. If they were to find out that they had helped Otto escape and hide then his dad's career would be over and Arnold would never be able to become a Doyen.

"I need to head back to the Chichen now, Mr. Whittaker wants my report on his desk by the end of the day.

Remember - lie low until I figure out what to do." With this, he left Arnold's bedroom and within a few moments, the house was empty, apart from the boys. Arnold went downstairs and made them both a ham sandwich and a drink of orange juice while they sat and discussed their next move. Arnold already knew where the best place for him to stay was. He just hoped that Otto felt the same.

"I have a lockup," Arnold started, "I don't know where it came from, but someone moved my grandad's things there."

"I know." Otto looked sheepish. "I followed you guys there and the last couple of times I have been there I've blacked out and transformed." Cutting a forlorn figure, Otto finished his sandwich and took a large gulp of his drink. "I feel famished. Transforming does take all my energy." Arnold felt amazed at how easily Otto was distracted, having shifted from following them at the lockup to being starving within the same sentence. It felt like he had his friend back which was fantastic. No matter how different he was physically, he was still Otto.

"My lock up - you can only get in and out with me, so if we get some supplies you can stay there and if you do change again, I'm pretty sure you won't be able to get out. It's the best we can do. What about your dad?"

"He knows I have been seen so he won't be expecting me, I won't tell him where I am."

They left Arnold's house and walked around the corner to Mr. Shah's shop to get some basic things for Otto for the rest of the weekend. They walked in and could smell the alluring scent of his freshly made samosas that lay by the side of the till. Mr. Shah did not sell these he simply gave them away throughout the day to his customers as a thank you for their custom. The shop was only small as it was initially a terraced house with Mr. Shah's family converting the front of it into a shop some years ago. Walking in, the shop felt cramped with shelves on either side of them and the counter directly in front. A rack lay just to the left-hand side of the counter, filled with a wide range of chocolate bars ranging from mars bars, snickers and, Arnold's personal favourite, mint aero. The two of them went to opposite sides of the store to collect things that they would need for the rest of the weekend. Arnold grabbed some chocolate bars and a couple of bags of crisps. There were tins of beans and other canned goods but the lockup did not have the facilities for cooking. It did, however, give Arnold food for thought about whether or not he would be able to upgrade the container so that it was more hospitable than its current state.

The two of them met at the counter with Otto having grabbed a couple of comics, some gum and far more fizzy drinks than he could ever drink. They bought their supplies and accepted a couple of Mr. Shah's samosas before carrying on to the lockup, taking extra care to ensure they were not being followed.

As they approached the courtyard to the lockup where his container was, it felt more like a desert; the heat from the sun was that intense. Arnold suddenly thought that maybe it wasn't such a bad thing that Otto had chosen to buy so many drinks. Having reached the container, Arnold placed his hand on the door to unlock the intricate mechanism that guarded his inherited belongings. Arnold opened up the door, the loud sound of metal grinding echoed through the grounds startling some birds that were perched on the outer perimeter wall. As the door opened, the heat from the container slapped Arnold in the face like a wet flannel. The air he breathed in felt hot and suddenly he had second thoughts about Otto staying in the container.

"I'm going to be like a dog left in a car, aren't I?" Otto sighed. "Except this car doesn't have any bloody windows." Feeling sorry for him, Arnold passed him a chocolate bar as a peace offering.

"It's the best we have at the moment." Otto looked around the container and gave an expression of disinterest in all the ancient texts and parchment that lay scattered around the room. He certainly did not share the same interest in reading that Arnold had. However, he did seem keen to look at the different artefacts and the small selection of weapons that were inside.

"I will stay as long as I can. That way, we won't need to shut the door." The truth was Arnold was worried Otto would not last long in the airtight sealed container in this heat. Otto appreciated this and took out one of the comics he had bought to skim through while Arnold continued to look through different books and tried to place things in some kind of order within the container.

Arnold's phone rang, it was Everett. He answered the call to let her know where he was. A short time later and the two of them were sat reading; Otto making his way through his comic and Arnold reading through his grandad's journal.

"Otto, what are you doing here? Would it have taken two seconds to let me know you were ok?" Everett stood at the entrance to the storage container. She was confused as to how the two of them were sat there as though nothing had happened when the last time she saw them, Otto had changed and attacked them before running off.

"You need to sit down. There is a lot to get through," Otto smiled.

Otto and Arnold spent the next hour explaining what had happened behind the shop with Everett listening intently. Once she was up to date, the three of them continued pottering about the container looking through more of his grandad's ancient texts. Arnold had found another handwritten journal which he was making his way through, this one acting more like a diary. It was amazing to be able to sit there reading his grandad's thoughts about different assignments and cases he had had during his time in the Chichen. Arnold had learned a lot about his life but never really anything like this. Certainly, nothing so personal that no one else had ever seen and it made him feel as though his grandad was still with him in some small way.

16th January 1985,

Life has not been the same since we lost her. I am unable to concentrate at work. Arthur has been acting out, asking where his mum is. He is too young for me to explain the complexities of what we had to do to trap her in the spirit world. It was by no means what I wanted, but the Chichen wished to capture her like she was some form of an animal. They would have used her like some lab rat and I could not let that happen. Eventually, she would have been killed and this was the only way to keep her alive and everyone else safe.

I have been tasked with looking into some intelligence that the Almec has resurfaced recently. This is the last thing the Chichen needs.

The last thing I need right now. Another day in the life of an Elder. How I do miss being a Doyen.

Hershel.

"You ok?" Everett asked as she stood looking at different items in the cupboard at the corner of the storage container. Taking an old bowl out and blowing the decades-old layer of dust that had collected on the top of it to reveal a decorative pattern underneath.

"I'm fine." Remembering that there were other people in the room, he shook his head before closing the journal and putting it back into the box it came from. He decided he would carry on reading it later when he was on his own. Arnold could feel himself welling up. Being able to read his grandad's thoughts resonated with Arnold even more than he had expected. He could only wish that his Grandad had told him all this in person.

CHAPTER 17

He stared up at the open sky as he attempted to draw his breath after falling to the bottom of the steep hill in an unknown land. He noticed the air was hot, burning his throat as he took short sharp breaths. He acclimatised himself to the pain he was experiencing all over his body. Not only had he fallen badly down this hill, but he had also been tortured by her and the dragon that controlled her. The sun was incredibly bright and he could see the occasional bird gliding in the sky above him. He could hear shuffling nearby and turned his head to see where the noise was coming from. His eyes were swollen from the beating and his vision was not the best, but he could see a beautiful young woman he saw staring down at him. Her dark skin shimmered in the sun and her long hair, decorated with beads and braids was stunning. His attention, however, was caught straight away by her big amber eyes which effortlessly held his gaze. Her smile was innocent as she tried to reassure him and when she knelt next to him, her softly spoken accent was not one that he had heard before.

"Are you ok?" she asked.

"I've had better days." The girl looked around the same age as him and as she helped him up, he instantly felt a connection between the two of them. He felt a strange knotted feeling in his stomach and he suddenly didn't know what to say. She stepped in front of him and pushed his hair to one side, noticing the large gash on his head was fresh and pouring with blood.

"You come with me?" She took hold of his hand and pulled him to follow her. Her hands felt soft to touch in comparison to the rough skin on his hands. "What's your name?"

"I don't have one." He was honest with her. He had met people before when he had travelled into this world and he knew other people had names. However, for him, he had merely been born; he was an item, a belonging. One that hadn't been nurtured or had the basic gift in life of receiving a name to give him an identity.

"No name?" The girl shook this off and continued the walk through the barren terrain. "My name is Kaliska. We go to my tribe. My father is a shaman. He can heal you," she reassured him as he was clearly in a daze and did not understand what was going on.

Kaliska had grown up with her tribe in harsh surroundings. He wondered how it must have felt to live and grow with a family, something which he had never had. The tribe lived within the trees which were a good ten-mile walk from where Kaliska has found him. In the time it took to reach the settlement, the two of them began to bond despite his head growing fuzzy through his injuries and dehydration. Kaliska stopped by a small running stream, allowing them both a short break and to rehydrate themselves. She sat him down on a rock and pooled some water in her hand. Kaliska wiped across his face to remove some of the blood that had dried around his swollen eyes. She paused for a moment, startled at the scars that were revealed from cleaning the blood away on his face, she slowly placed her fingers at the top of them before gently tracing the natural cracks that had formed across his eye and face. "How?"

He turned his head away, feeling like a freak and uncomfortable with anyone being so intimate with his scars. He felt hideous and he hated the scars that he had been forced to receive when he was so young. A memory that was etched into his mind. A memory that would often wake him in the night with cold sweats when he was experiencing night terrors. Kaliska turned his head back to face hers and smiled at him. He could not understand why she was so kind to him.

"You grow with your scars. You accept your scars; they are part of you. You grow stronger." She was not disgusted by his disfigurement in any way and softly cupped his cheek. "We are not far now, come." She took hold of his hand again. He followed her until eventually they made it to a heavily forested area.

They continued their journey through the dense wood before eventually they reached her village. "This is home." There were a series of huts dotted around with him able to count about ten from where he was standing. The huts were made from a combination of wood, mud and large leaves from the trees. There was one larger hut that sat at the top of the village and in the centre lay a large shelter that everyone in the village used as a communal space. This was where rituals and meetings would be conducted between the older and more experienced village folk. Most importantly, it was where everyone sat at night to eat, together as one community, one family unit.

He instantly felt at home and fell in love with the environment, enjoying being in a populated area where it was not overcrowded. There was no trading, no one trying to get richer than the others. Everyone did their bit to contribute to the village and everything was shared equally. Greed did not exist here and it was so refreshing for him to see a purity rather than what he was accustomed to seeing when he usually found himself in this world.

Following Kaliska, he could see different people busy getting on with their day. There was a group of women walking back to camp carrying water and some men were working on the roof of one of the huts, pulling a large leaf over the top of a small gap. Children were running around chasing after each other, laughing and smiling at one another. No-one stopped to look at the stranger that had walked into their village with Kaliska and most notably, no one had stopped to gawp at the scars on his face. Kaliska pushed open the door to a large hut that sat at the back of the village overlooking all the other huts. The door opened and the two of them walked inside. The hut was poorly lit with only a couple of candles providing any form of lighting. He could see the frame of a man sitting in a tall chair, his face half-covered from the shadows in the hut.

"Father," Kaliska started. "I bring this man to be healed."

Picking up a torch, the shaman walked in front of him and began to look him up and down, taking in every detail of him like he was a builder surveying a blueprint. "I sense great pain and anguish." The shaman placed a firm hand on his shoulder, the lines on his face showing he was slightly older than he would have expected to have a daughter of Kaliska's age. He instantly felt more relaxed and calmer and strangely his throbbing head and aching body began to fade to a dull ache.

"Come, sit." He gestured to the chair that he had been sat on when the two of them had entered. Feeling obligated to do so, he limped across to the chair and took a seat as directed. "Fetch my things, Kaliska." She disappeared into the darkness of the hut and returned with a satchel. She passed it to the shaman before nodding to him and leaving the hut. The shaman walked over to him and stared at his head for a moment before pulling out a tiny metal hook. "This needs sealing." He pointed to the top of his head before pointing to the hook he had in his hand. "First, it needs cleaning."

At this point, Kaliska returned with a bowl of water and some dressings which she began to use to clean the open wound. He didn't flinch as she scrubbed at the gash in his head. The pain was minimal compared to what he had been through in his past. After cleaning his head, she stepped back to allow the shaman to approach again, this time with some thread in the hook. Carefully, he pierced his skin as he began to stitch the torn skin back together. After a short while, the stitches were done and the Shaman walked to a small table and picked up a pestle and mortar made of wood and stone. He began to grind different herbs together until he formed a thick green paste which he then scooped up in his hands and smeared over the freshly sealed gash. "Kaliska, dress his head and meet me outside." He walked away from them and left the hut, leaving them alone inside.

Kaliska began to delicately wrap a dressing around his head. His heart fluttered as she stood over him; he had never been this close to a girl before and he didn't know where to look or what to do so he sat there feeling awkward.

"Your cut should be healed in the next week or two." She placed her hand on his cheek once more, rubbing her thumb over the bottom of his three sizeable claw mark scars that left deep indentations in his skin. Her sensitivity and soft hands calmed him even further and for a moment he did wonder whether or not she had the same healing abilities as her father. In that moment, he didn't feel sad or empty and he certainly didn't feel lonely. He also didn't feel pain for the first time since he had met her. At this moment, all he felt was happiness.

"Come." Kaliska turned to leave the hut and he quickly followed outside. A small gathering had formed around the large shelter in the middle of the village. The shaman stood in the centre, waving his hands around while he conversed with the villagers that stood around him. He followed Kaliska over to the central shelter and he was summoned up by the shaman. "Tell me, what is your name?"

"He has no name," Kaliska shouted out from within the crowd that had formed. Gasps rang out around them. It was most strange for them to meet someone in his teenage years that did not have a name.

"Interesting, tell me what is your spirit beast?"

"Lions," he answered, not wanting to go into the complexities of what had happened earlier that day with the blade he had stolen. The shaman began humming and chanting to himself while he poured a mixture of herbs and liquids into a bowl before passing it to him to hold.

"Drink." Lifting the bowl, he drank the contents and was pleasantly surprised by the sweet taste, similar to honey. Certainly not the bitterness he had braced himself for. The shaman closed his eyes and began to chant once more. "The spirits, they speak to me," he whispered. "They say your name, your name means lion. It means brave and honoured. It means protector." He walked across to him and placed both his hands on his shoulders and squeezed them both tightly. He had never felt so welcomed anywhere and he wished he could stay here for the rest of his life. He bowed his head to the shaman as a mark of respect to him. "Your name is Levent."

Finally having a name and an identity, Levent felt on top of the world and over the next few months, he became ingrained as a member of the tribe. He spent a large portion of his time out with other members of the tribe, developing his hunting skills and providing for the village by catching and killing wild animals that lived around the forest. It was his way of contributing to the village that had accepted him with open arms and offered such kindness to a stranger in need. He felt prepared to spend the rest of his life repaying them. This was the safest he had ever felt and he finally had somewhere where he could call home. They had helped to build his own hut within the village where he had stored his blade away, not wanting to share that it was through this weapon that he was able to summon a spirit beast in case they treated him any differently. He was happy.

On this day, he had helped capture a wild boar which had been hogtied around a large wooden pole and carried back to the settlement. This boar was large enough to feed the entire village for at least two days and that night, while the boar roasted on a spit, the village celebrated their life and their family before all sitting down together to feast.

Feeling full from his share of the boar, Levent decided to call it a night and headed back to his hut to get some rest. His injuries had healed well and the scar on his head was now barely noticeable. Having acquired the boar, he knew there would be no need for hunting the next day and so he wanted to make sure he got a good night's sleep. He planned to have a good exploration of the nearby areas, something he had not done since he had arrived. He quietly made his way back to his hut to not cause any offence for leaving early and managed to get there unseen. He stepped inside and sighed. He was tired after today's work and could not wait to get in bed.

He heard something and realised that he was not alone in the hut, turning to his side to see what the noise was that startled him. A shadowed figure ran towards him and Levent braced himself. To his relief, it was Kaliska who wrapped her arms around him and the two of them shared a warm embrace before sharing a kiss.

"I missed you today," she whispered.

"I missed you, too." They continued to kiss for a while, enjoying the moment while they could. They had been meeting up like this for six weeks now, in the darkness away from everyone else.

"I need to speak with your father. I can ask his permission," Levent said.

"I'm not eighteen yet. Be patient. He will allow it but not until then. He is bound by the rules of the tribe." She kissed him on the cheek and left the hut, turning to smile at him before she left. Levent lay down on his bed and let out a huge sigh. He hated having to hide this. He just wanted to be honest with everyone in the village, to be honest with the man who had welcomed him into the tribe with open arms. He was in love with the shaman's daughter.

CHAPTER 18

It was six o'clock. Arnold was heading to the Chichen; he always went on a Saturday at some point and with everything that had been going on, he didn't want to draw attention to himself by not going today. Everett had already headed home and Arnold had secured Otto in the container. He was starting to get nervous because Otto's dad, Mayor Redburn, had not been in contact, demanding to know where he was. This was something they had been expecting given that everyone had seen the were-jaguar in town; they just weren't aware that it was Otto.

Arnold had explained he was going to the Chichen as per usual and then heading back to the container afterwards. This was the best thing they could think of to keep Otto safe should he transform; he would be in a secure place and only Arnold could get in, given that the locking mechanism could only be activated by his auro.

The sun was beginning to set and the temperature was cooling which was something that he had been grateful for as Otto was now holed up in the airtight storage container. He arrived at the Chichen and headed straight to the changing room to get dressed in his training clothes. His plan was to train until eight and then head back. When

Arnold came out of the changing rooms, the Chichen seemed unusually quiet. Usually, he would be able to hear his dad or some of the other Doyens around, but today it appeared empty. Arnold headed back to the reception and noticed that Grace wasn't sat at the reception and thinking back, he couldn't recall if she had been sat at her desk when he entered.

Arnold headed to the training room and started training with his macuahuitl. It wasn't the best training session he had ever had, given that he could not concentrate today. Arnold took a short break before putting away the macuahuitl and working on his physical strength, making his way through a routine of press-ups, sit-ups, squats and planking. He had developed so much physically over the last year. Arnold now had definitive muscles that had formed all over his body; he had been training hard and could see the changes it had made to him. He felt so much fitter and stronger than when he started training at the Chichen.

After finishing up with his exercises, he was packing up when he saw the hilts his dad had used with him when they were practising spirit wielding. He thought for a moment before deciding he would have another try at the spirit wielding. He picked up the hilt and focused his energy, concentrating like his dad had told him too, time and time again. Each time that he had tried, he had failed but for some reason, he felt more confident this time. He continued to focus and his hands began to glow with his auro. His hand started to tingle, then he fell to the floor convulsing as though he had just stuck his finger into a plug socket. All his muscles tensed tightly as raw sprit energy coursed through his body. It was a horrible experience, but Arnold knew he needed to get his body used to the spirit energy. Previously his dad had assured him that each time he did this process, it would hurt a little less as his body became used to the process. At this moment in time, however, as Arnold lay convulsing on the cold floor once more, he did not feel as though anything felt easier than last time. He was struggling to concentrate on getting up from the floor. Then, to Arnold's amazement, he felt like he had some control over his body and he began to climb to his feet, his muscles still tensed up tightly. He managed to stand up though it took everything he had not to allow his body to fold in on itself and slam him back against the floor. He was determined to do this. He managed to hold his ground for two seconds before he crumpled up on the floor again, letting go of the hilt to break the connection, allowing him the release of not having the raw energy flow through him. He panted on the floor as he regained his breath and waited for his muscles to stop tingling before getting back to his feet.

He stared at the hilt before shaking his head at his disbelief. Arnold knew how much of a glutton for punishment he had become. He picked it up and went through this process repeatedly, each time managing to climb to his feet and stay on his feet that tiny bit longer until the point where he felt as though he couldn't practice anymore. He lay on the floor, having decided he had had enough practice today, with a real sense of accomplishment and feeling happy with the progress that he had made. Once his muscles had stopped tingling, he put away the training weapons before having a large drink of water. His body was now feeling slightly jittery and a little bit numb from his overexertion. He went back to the changing room and got showered and dressed before heading to the exit.

He walked through reception and it was still oddly silent. Arnold looked down the corridor at the training room and towards the exit and a thought went through his head. He stopped walking and headed back to the training room and opened the weapon's room and picked up his macuahuitl blade. With everything going on, he felt like he would be that little bit safer if he had this with him. No one was around to stop him taking it out of the Chichen, so Arnold fastened its holster over his shoulder. He then put the macuahuitl against it and quickly headed back down the corridor and left the Chichen. Arnold knew he would be in trouble if he got caught, so he kept his head down and kept walking at a fast pace until he was well away from the Chichen and out of sight.

He headed back to the Bramley lock-up so that he could ensure Otto got some fresh air as he had been inside for a couple of hours now. He reached the container and looked forward to sitting down and resting. He felt exhausted. Placing his hand on the side he felt it begin to tingle and the container opened up.

"How are you-?" Arnold stopped his sentence as he opened the door to the container to reveal that it was empty. Otto was not there. Arnold quickly looked around. Nothing seemed misplaced, nor did it look like there had been any form of a struggle. Otto had simply vanished into thin air. Arnold pulled out his phone and rang Otto, but he didn't answer. Arnold continued to survey the container when he noticed something perched against the cabinet at the side of the container. Walking across, he picked it up to see a card not too dissimilar to a business card. He turned it over to reveal a print of an old picture. Arnold recognised the image straight away. It was the head of a were-jaguar. Arnold had seen this symbol somewhere before and he grabbed his grandad's journal straight away. He flipped it to the page about the were-jaguar and there it was. The same picture that was on the card was in his grandad's book. Next to the picture was the description of who had taken Otto. It was the Almec; whoever they were they had Otto and they wanted Arnold to find them. Why else would they leave this card here? The next moment, Arnold felt darkness, his head was covered from behind and his arms grabbed to stop him from moving.

"Do not be afraid." A softly spoken woman's voice spoke from behind him. "Relax, we have your friend. Come with us." Arnold relaxed his muscles, knowing he didn't have much choice. He followed in the direction that he was being taken before he felt himself be put into a car which set off, taking him to another destination. He felt wedged in the car with someone sat either side of him. He tried to tip his head back to improve his vision, but whatever had been put over his head ensured he couldn't see anything. He sat in silence, choosing not to speak. He was pretty confident he knew who it was that had crept up on him, given the card he had been left in the storage container. He sat calmly and quietly in the car before eventually, it pulled up somewhere and the engine stopped.

The door opened and suddenly the pressure to his right side left as that person got out of the vehicle. The same person grabbed hold of his arm and led him out of the car. Arnold listened intently to the surroundings and could hear running water, like a stream. He followed the guidance he was being given before coming to an abrupt stop. Arnold could still hear the stream a little but could not feel any breeze on him, which indicated to him that he was indoors somewhere. Shortly after stopping, the hood that had been placed over him was removed and Arnold squinted as he became accustomed to the light.

The room he was in was large and hollow with Arnold quickly realising he was in some form of a warehouse. He couldn't help but notice the smell of chemicals that faintly hung in the air. The scent reminded him of hospitals.

Arnold looked around the room and could see a group of men and women stood around him in a large circle; each had different animal hides that they were each wearing like hoods. All of them was dressed in some form of armour that resembled bone mail, intricately bound together somehow. There were many shapes and sizes stood around him, noticeably two large, well-built men that Arnold presumed he had been sat between in the car on his way here. His bleary eyes drew back to the masked figure that stood in front of him. He knew it was a woman by her delicate shape; however, he could not see her face due to it being covered with the hide of a jaguar. This all but confirmed to Arnold who he was dealing with.

"Are you-?"

"The Almec? Yes," she answered, her voice reassuring and soothing. Her long white gown draping down to the floor where she stood. She had her hands resting in front of her, her slender fingers interlocking between one another.

"Where's Otto?" Arnold asked.

"He is fine. We have given him something that should help him with his transition into Night-Sun. Make it less painful in the future."

"What do you want with him?"

"For him to be safe and free from control," she explained to Arnold. Her voice was so gentle.

"Then we want the same thing," Arnold responded.

"We have been observing you for a while now, Arnold Ethon. Your loyalty and dedication to Night-Sun is to be admired." She was impressed with Arnold and what he stood for. "Your grandfather would be proud."

Her words piqued Arnold's interest instantly.

"You knew my grandad?" he asked, their conversation suddenly becoming more interesting. The woman stood before him nodded.

"Yes, we did. Who do you think moved all his belongings to the lock-up for you?" This did not make any sense to Arnold. Why on earth would they have moved all the items from the loft to a storage container?

"Why?"

"Because he willed us to do so, Arnold."

"What do you mean?" His confusion was growing. "Why would he ask for that?" The woman stepped forward, taking hold of Arnold's hands to reassure him.

"Your grandfather was a good man like you are becoming. He came to see me shortly before he died and requested that if his time came, we remove his belongings. He wanted us to put them somewhere safe before the Chichen took them." Arnold felt even more confused now; how did his grandad know them and why would he not want the Chichen to get hold of his items? "You have his journal, do you not?" Arnold nodded. "Then I recommend you read it to get some insight. That journal was always intended for you. Your grandfather wanted to explain. For me to do so would be disrespectful of his wishes and all that he stood for." The two solidly built men stepped forward and covered Arnold's head once more and placed the hood over him. "We wanted to reveal ourselves to you to show we exist. We will keep Night-Sun safe, Arnold. You can trust us. More than you can trust the Chichen." With this, the woman placed some salts underneath Arnold's nose, which he inhaled and began to slip into unconsciousness. "Do not be afraid. We will guide you home, Arnold Ethon." With this, Arnold drifted away into the darkness.

Arnold's dream took over and he found himself stood in the same warehouse but instead of people stood around him in a circle, he was surrounded by different spirit animals. In front of him stood a coyote, to the left of him a wolf and a hyena. To his right was a reindeer and a buffalo, all of which stood staring, entirely focused on him. He went to move his arms and noticed that they were wings; he was in his eagle form. Stretching out his wings, the surrounding animals began to buck and bow their heads towards him. Arnold felt as though they were saluting him, giving him the nod to say that they approved of him. He could not help but think that these were the spirit beasts of the people that had been stood around him in the warehouse. It was the most bizarre dream.

When he woke up, Arnold found that he was in his bed and he couldn't help but wonder if the night before had just been a dream. He felt a little dehydrated and sat up in bed to see a glass of water next to his bed with the card from the Almec balanced against it, confirming that last night had indeed happened. He sat there, processing everything that had been said and then began to wonder how they had got him back to his bed without anyone noticing. Then again, they had managed to move everything from his grandad's to the lock-up without being seen so that shouldn't really surprise him. The woman had told him to read his grandad's journal and not to trust the Chichen. Arnold felt that the woman had guided him and knew that in reading the journal, he would begin to understand what she had meant. How could he not trust the Chichen though? It was all he had ever known or wanted and he was being trained by them. Why would his grandad have been working with the Almec? Arnold looked at his alarm clock. It was four am and he was exhausted, his head was spinning and his body was aching. Arnold remembered that he had left the journal at the storage container and he planned on going there to read it. First, he needed to rest for a few more hours at least.

CHAPTER 19

Levent woke to a shrill scream and his heart instantly began racing. He jumped out of his bed at speed and headed out from his hut to see what was happening. He could see different members of the tribe had begun to emerge from their huts, some of whom had brought their weapons with them. Looking across the settlement, he could see some strangers stood in the shelter in the middle of the village. They looked hostile and he could see the shaman knelt on the floor in front of them facing away from them as though he was on parade.

Levent ran back into his hut, reached underneath his bed and pulled out a roll of fabric that lay there collecting dust. He quickly unwrapped the cloth to reveal his ebony and ivory blade. Grabbing hold of it, he stood up and tucked it into the back of his pants before exiting the hut once more.

"This is what happens when you defy the will of the Chichen!" a voice called from behind the shaman. "Now, I suggest that if you want your shaman to live, then you will stand before us and listen to what we have to offer." Levent shuffled up before the crowd that had started to form around the shelter and could see that one of the three men had hold of Kaliska. It was her scream that had caused

Levent and the rest of the tribe to wakeup. He wanted to rush forward to help them but knew what the consequences might be if he did. He had no choice but to listen to what they had to say. Seeing Kaliska in danger like this made him angry. It was a wave of the old anger he had managed to keep suppressed for some time, he didn't want to release it but he would if he had to.

"We have come to believe that there may be some artefacts here," the man in the middle shouted. He was wearing his sandy coloured pants and green khaki t-shirt, his sweat forming a wet v down the front of it such was the humidity. "You should be aware that the Chichen has issued orders to collect such artefacts to preserve safety for all."

"You wish only to preserve yourselves!" an older man called from within the crowd, prompting some of the other tribesmen to cheer. The man laughed to himself before stepping forward and hitting the shaman in the back of the head, knocking him forward.

"See what you made me do?" he goaded. "Now I don't want to come in here and have to start roughing people up. Just give me what we have been sent here for. I am going to ask this once and once only. If there are any artefacts here, you have ten minutes to find them and bring them to us before we take things further."

"Give it to him, Kaliska," the shaman called, "No one needs to get hurt."

"But father!"

"No!" His voice was stern and full of authority. "It is my choice." Kaliska pulled away from the man holding her. The leader of the group nodded for him to let go to allow her to fetch what they had come here for. She disappeared into the shaman's hut before returning with a chalice which she held tightly to her chest as she walked back up to them.

"Father, we can't let them-" Before she could finish her sentence, she was slapped to the floor by one of the men. He had been the one holding her just a short time before. He laughed out loud to himself and groans of disapproval rang out from the tribe. The leader knelt to her level and lifted her head to look him in the eyes.

"Now, don't be putting ideas in the old man's head. I'm sure he just told you to hand it over to me." As he said this, a tremendous roar erupted from the darkness and the crowd parted between them and the shelter. Levent stood there with his fists tightly clenched. In his right hand, he was holding his dagger. Either side of him stood the two giant mane-less lions which stood on all fours and were ready to strike at any moment. An orange auro emitting from the dagger and around the spirit beast and Levent's hand glowed where he clenched his dagger tightly. Their roars echoed around the village, forcing some of the other villagers to shriek out in fear. He was furious at the way the Shaman and Kaliska were being treated and he would not allow these intruders to stay here any longer. He would not let them take from the tribe anything that was not theirs.

"How dare you!" he growled. "You strike down Kaliska and our shaman! You dishonour whoever you represent." With this, his two lions set off running through the crowd and leapt through the air instantly pinning the leader's henchmen to the floor, staring them dead in the eyes. They looked willing to bite down on their prey; all Levent needed to do was will it and it would be done. Levent however, only had eyes for one person and he ran towards the shelter himself, striking out at the leader and letting out a roar of anger. The leader dodged this and pulled out his blade. He lunged forward and attempted to slice Levent, but he blocked this with his blade before striking out with his free hand against the leader's face. The man was twice his age and the strength of Levent's punch surprised him.

"You are stronger than you look, boy." He lashed out again with his knife which Levent dodged with ease before striking back, this time with his elbow and knocked the leader down to his knees. He kicked out, knocking the leader's knife out of his hand before quickly holding his blade to the man's neck, hard enough to cause a slight cut to his throat.

"Get your men and leave," he growled at them. His breathing was heavy, his aggression rising.

"And if we don't?" The leader smirked, his arrogance unbearable.

Levent knew that his patience was running out and his frustration was becoming dangerously close to bubbling over right in front of everybody. The smaller of the two lions let out a roar and lunged forward, biting down on the thug that it had pinned to the floor. He let out an ear curdling scream as the lion's teeth pierced his flesh and started to shake his head. The leader looked at him and seemed equally angry.

"Fine, we will leave," he fumed. Levent's lion instantly stopped its attack and the two of them stepped away from their prey so they could return to their feet. Levent moved away from the leader, allowing him to climb to his feet before pushing him across the shelter to his thugs. The three of them gathered themselves before they set off to leave with their tail between their legs. Levent turned to help the shaman back up to his feet. He had remained silent during the exchange between him and the invaders.

"That blade, where did you get that blade?"

"I've always had it." His lie was easier than explaining how he had stolen it while in the spirit world.

"I know it. I know that blade." He seemed as sure as he was that the sun comes out during the day. Levent felt confused, thinking he must be mistaken. There was no way that he could have recognised the blade that he had in his possession. He had spent his entire life in the spirit world and he had only acquired the blade just before being transported here. His mother had always had it in her possession, going back as far as he could remember.

"My great grandfather, he is the one who created that artefact. He is the one who controlled the lions of Tsavo." The shaman reached out for the blade wanting to look at it more closely. "May I?" Levent passed him the blade not wanting to cause any offence, but he did feel uncomfortable not knowing whether or not the shaman would give it back since it appeared to be a long lost family air loom. "This is by no means a coincidence. This blade has connected to you. You have no idea the power you possess because of this blade."

"Can you show me?" Levent asked, wanting to know as much as he could about the blade.

"You have shown great courage and restraint in fending off those Chichen invaders. They roam the lands removing artefacts and hiding them away in London. They don't want any menials to wield their power. They are purists."

"I think I am a menial; without that blade, I have no spirit beast," Levent explained.

"That may be so. Without your soul, the lions of Tsavo would not have anyone to connect within this world. They need you as much as you need them." The shaman passed the blade back to Levent. "This is yours. The spirits wanted you to be here at this time, at this moment. To protect us." Levent took the blade back from the shaman and an overwhelming sense of pride overpowered his emotions. He finally had a purpose and he knew that from this day on he would protect this tribe and its people from the Chichen.

Weeks turned to months and months turned to years and before Levent knew it, twelve years had passed and he had become a central pillar within the tribe. His dark hair had grown long, his skin had become tanned and his torturous past was just a distant memory. He had escaped that life and found himself in his version of paradise one, that he never wanted to leave. He had been the protector of the tribe and his ability to summon two-spirit beasts had become legendary in the region, ensuring that no outsiders had stepped foot within the tribe while he had been there. They had remained safe and undisturbed, able to live peacefully. Levent had spent his time with the shaman who had been training him for the last twelve years. The shaman's plan was for Levent to step into his shoes once he passed.

Levent had become even stronger and through his hunting, gathering and general work within the community, he had developed a muscular physique. His training had been intense at times, but Levent had become masterful at wielding his spirit blade. He had been told its correct name was the blade of the spirits, but Levent much preferred the shortened name he had become accustomed to using; he found that it rolled off the tongue much easier. He had lost count of the hours he must have spent training with the weapon. The shaman had told him that to truly master the blade he would need to have practised with it more than ten thousand hours. Levent felt that he must have been close to this figure as he had practised every single day with it for the entire time he had been with the tribe. His combat ability was his strength and he had proven to be the strongest and most skilled in the tribe. However, he was not yet skilled enough in the arts needed to be a shaman. He needed to be able to heal using his spirit beasts. He needed to learn all the different remedies and potions that the shaman had developed and created himself. The shaman had even told him that one day when he had mastered his powers and abilities, he would be able to create artefacts himself. This was the highest skill a shaman could achieve and took an incredible amount of energy to be able to do it, the reason why shamans avoided it because, for each time they did, their life expectancy would shorten.

The shaman had always told him he wasn't ready to learn this skill yet and that ultimately he would only show him reluctantly so that the power was passed on within the tribe. Being close to the shaman, it had become Levent's role to be involved in decision making and the rest of the people that lived in this community had nothing but respect for him. Levent was kind, caring and compassionate but the thing he was admired for was his bravery which he had demonstrated time and time again, putting other people's safety before his own. It was through this bravery that the shaman had given his blessing to him marrying his daughter, Kaliska. The two of them had been in a relationship for twelve years now and Levent was still as devoted to his daughter now as the day he discovered that they had begun to see one another.

Levent stood in his hut with two other members of the tribe. They were painting his body with different colours, creating symbols and drawings and within this was a hieroglyph of his spirit beasts and Kaliska's. One of the tribesmen picked up a sash and placed this over the top of his head. It rested against his shoulders. The leaves which formed part of the sash felt as though it was scratching his skin, but he was quickly able to ignore this.

"Are you ready?" The tribesman asked, his body also decorated in different colours. He was already prepared for the occasion.

"It is what I have always wanted." He was feeling incredibly nervous, the most nervous he had ever felt. His stomach was tied up in knots and he felt as though he could vomit at any moment.

Today was a special day. Today he was going to marry the love of his life, Kaliska.

CHAPTER 20

As soon as Arnold had wok up, he got himself dressed and headed down to the lockup. He was on a mission to read through his grandad's journal just like the woman had told him to do the night before. It wasn't as warm today as it had been the day before, with the weather appearing slightly overcast as the clouds sitting low on the hills that sat towards the far side of Oswald. As he left his house, he could barely see the wind turbines that sat atop using the force of the wind to generate power for their town. Not all of them appeared to be moving, but then the wind did not feel that strong today. The town was eerily quiet with it being so early on a Sunday and Arnold couldn't remember the last time that he had been up this early and out of the house at the weekend. His eyes were still bleary and he wiped the dry sleep that had crusted underneath his eyelid, causing his eyes to water even more.

By now he had become used to the aching feeling all over his body from his physical training and training to spirit wield, but today he could not help but feel that he had pushed himself too far the day before. As he made his way through the ghost-like town, he could see one of the many cafés that populated Oswald was opening. The woman that owned it was setting everything up in the back of the open plan kitchen while one of the waitresses stood outside having a cigarette. The newspaper boy was exiting the newspaper shop next door, with his large paper bag looking fit to burst. The paperboy looked over-encumbered, as though he could fall at any moment. He placed his paper bag in between himself and the handlebars of his bike while shuffling along with his feet. Apart from the café workers and the paperboy, Arnold didn't see anyone else on his way over to the lockup. By the time he reached it he felt like the fresh air had cleared his lungs and he felt revitalised.

He opened his lockup and could see his grandfather's journal sat on the side of the cupboard where he had left it. He grabbed the leather book and hastily opened it. Wanting to learn what the woman had meant by what she had said to him. He skipped past the entry he had read the night before and started to read the next entries one by one. It was fascinating to read, with each entry explaining the work his grandad had been carrying out for the Chichen and getting to travel all across the world in the process. Stories ranged from stopping robberies, thugs and even a murder in the early nineties. Each entry he read showed how great his grandad had been as a Doyen and then later on in his career as the Elder.

Making his way through the journal, one entry caught his attention as he spotted a reference to the Almec.

April 15th, 1995

I don't like the way the Chichen store artefacts and keep them menials from using them. It just does not sit right. And how the Chichen has acquired some artefacts have been questionable. It's why I have always stored some at home. I honestly don't know whose hands are the wrong hands. Is it anyone wanting to use these artefacts, or is it the Chichen? I've recently had contact from the Almec. They are going to be here soon and have asked me to meet up with them. They had requested the artefact that I borrowed from them when we trapped Helen in the spirit world. I will have to speak to Edith. Hopefully, she will tell me where it is. After all, I did ask her to put it somewhere safe, in a location unknown to me.

The Almec and the Chichen… dare I write it but I feel more drawn towards the Almec at this moment in time. Maybe it's time I resigned as Elder. Something in their letter I received concerned me, they spoke of the Chichen crossing the line but did not tell me how. I am going to do some digging and see what I can find out before the Almec arrives.

Hershel Ethon

Arnold put the journal down to process what he had just read. It certainly came across to him that his grandad was not entirely on board with the Chichen. If that was the case, why had he never said anything to his dad or himself for that matter? Arnold had always wanted to join the Chichen, to become a Doyen and protect his community as his grandad had done. Like his dad still did. He felt incredibly confused and a little bit angry towards his grandad for not being honest with him. If he had, would he still have wanted to join the Chichen?

The containers door moved, startling Arnold. He jumped to his feet but quickly settled when he realised who it was. It was Marrok.

"Why are you here so early?" Marrok asked as he pulled the container door to the side, the metal scraped on the rollers echoing loudly around the isolated lock up.

"I was just going to ask you the same thing," Arnold said.

"What are you doing?" Arnold was still holding his grandad's journal and feeling his frustrations rising. He threw it down on the side. "Well, I was reading." He spoke shortly. "You might want to read that." Arnold pointed almost accusingly at the journal.

"What does it say?"

"Basically, my grandad didn't fully trust the Chichen and was looking to get out." Arnold sat perched against the cupboard the entire time, his frustration towards his grandad ever-growing. Why couldn't he have just been honest with him? What was he hiding? Arnold bombarded himself with more and more questions, his irritation beginning to fill his head.

"Right, ok…"Marrok's body language was not looking comfortable, which immediately caught Arnold's attention

"Everything ok? You seem…edgy?" Marrok shuffled about awkwardly rummaging through some old books that were in a box in front of him. "I'm fine, I mean your grandad might have had a reason for wanting to leave the Chichen. Maybe the Almec had more information and that's why they wanted to meet up." Arnold continued to watch Marrok, who was squirming that much he looked as though he was about to spontaneously combust.

"I didn't say anything about the Almec wanting to meet up with him." Arnold realised that he knew his friend was not being entirely honest with him, something he did not care to entertain today especially not after learning of his grandad's dishonesty about the Chichen. Arnold suddenly had a flashback a detail in the dream he had had last night which he had overlooked until now. Now it all made sense.

"You were there." When he had dreamt that he was surrounded by spirit animals, the one to his immediate left was a wolf, a white wolf. Arnold had thought nothing of this at the time given that a few spirit beasts surrounded him, but now it stood out to him like a sore thumb. How had he not picked this up any sooner? "You are with the Almec, aren't you?"

Marrok nodded, confirming Arnold's theory. "Yes." He put it as simply as he could. His nervousness subsided as soon as he spoke. He was finally unburdened of the secret he had been hiding from his new friend.

Arnold felt so disappointed that he had been lied to this entire time. It felt like he had just received a double blow of people not being honest with him and it hurt.

"Why? Why lie to me this whole time? Why not tell me why you were here?"

"I'm sorry, Arnold, I really am. I was following instructions. Trust me. I wanted to tell you everything."

"Trust you?" Arnold barked back. He was less than

impressed with Marrok's explanation; blaming someone else was the easy way out in his eyes. "Why? Why follow me all this time?" Arnold felt furious at the betrayal and could tell he was losing his temper. First his grandad and then his newest friend, both with connections to the Almec who had suddenly come forward to contact him yesterday. Arnold's world had been tipped upside down overnight and he was struggling to process all this new information.

"They wanted to make sure of your allegiance."

"My allegiance? I'm training at the Chichen. I want to be a Doyen. I'm going to be a Doyen."

"You need to calm down, Arnold. Let me explain," Marrok pleaded.

"Calm down!?" Arnold stood up and stepped towards Marrok to push past him.

Marrok stood his ground and pushed Arnold back into the container. "You need to listen to me."

Arnold felt incensed and his blood was rushing to his head. His anger was dangerously close to spilling over.

"Arnold, calm down. I am not here to hurt you. I am here to help you." His hands were up showing his open palms, trying to de-escalate the situation.

"What on earth is going on?" Everett scolded from outside the container. She stood with George by the side of her. Both of them were still wearing pyjamas with their coats over the top of them.

"We only came down because Everett saw you power walking through town," George yawned.

"Looks like it's a good job that we did. You look ready to kill someone." Everett's words were directed at Arnold, who stood inside the container with both his hands tightly clenched.

"Why don't you ask him? He's been lying to us this whole time. He is with the Almec. They have Otto!"

"Well right now you look like the only one capable of hurting anyone so sit down, shut up and let Marrok explain," Everett said assertively, her arms tightly folded.

Arnold sighed and reluctantly sat down. He didn't want to fight in front of Everett and George and opted to do as he had been told. He began to breathe in and out through his nose slowly to calm himself down.

"Fine. This had better be good, though." He sulked like a petulant child, folded his arms and waited to hear what lies would be spouted next. Marrok looked at Everett, amazed at her ability to calm Arnold down the way she had just done and smiled at her in appreciation at her help. However, Everett looked less than impressed and had a face like thunder as she stood there scowling at the pair of them. George shuffled into the container and sat herself down and placed her head against the container wall. She appeared distant and not that interested in what was going on.

"As I was trying to say, I was told that I was not allowed to tell you that I am part of the Almec. As you know, we have the belief that one day our deity would return in the form of the were-jaguar or, as we know him, Night-Sun. Something has happened to Otto. His body has somehow fused with that of his spirit beast which has given him the ability to transform himself into the were-jaguar."

"So, you think he is Night-Sun?" Everett asked.

"That is correct. We received information from Otto's family, who explained that he had become corrupted. We were sent to observe and I was sent in to get closer to Otto. I thought the best way of doing this was through you guys. My plan had taken longer than I expected, given that you two were not talking when I arrived here in Oswald. The Almec were concerned and we needed to trust that you would do right by Otto when you discovered his true identity. As expected, you did not fail and you have satisfied the council that you share your grandad's compassion for others."

"What do you know of my grandad?" Arnold pressed his body language indicating that he was still angry and his tone distinctly abrupt.

"That he was a kind man, just as you are. He saved us;

there are not many of the Almec left and the only reason we are still around is because of him. He came to see us shortly before he passed. He told us that you were being allowed to join the Chichen and this caused him great conflict. Do you remember Arnold? It was when he and your dad had fallen out?"

Arnold thought back to the argument he had heard between his grandad and his dad at his house in the middle of the night. The night that he had met Levent for the first time and rescued Charles Grey, a retired Doyen, one of the people involved in banishing his corrupted Grandma to the spirit world.

"I remember. Are you saying that when he left for a while, he was with the Almec?"

"Yes. That is exactly what I am saying. Your grandad asked us to do this for you when he was gone. To bring all of his belongings that he had collected through the years to safety here. So that you could keep them and learn from them. So that the Chichen would not take them for themselves."

"Why was he so against the Chichen when he dedicated his whole life to them?" Arnold could feel himself beginning to calm down. He was not fully there but his fists were now unclenched. He was, however, as confused as ever about what he was being told.

"I don't know all the answer's Arnold, but there are people from the Almec that do. People who knew your grandad far better than I ever did. Please, you need to work with us like your grandad once did."

"How do you mean?" George finally picked up on the conversation and had decided she would give her input.

"Something is happening, deep beneath us. There is a great amount of spirit energy within Oswald and it is coming from a gateway, one that was opened when your Grandma was sent there for her safety. We know that Mayor Redburn wants to open the mines beneath the town and delve deep enough to open a gateway to bring her back, we can't let that happen. Mayor Redburn is now in possession of an artefact which can be used to help open the gateway. He took it from your granny's shop, George." He turned to look at George as he delivered this information. George sat upright rather than leaning against a wall, suddenly looking very interested in Marrok's words. "But Otto broke in when he changed into the were-jaguar."

"Otto may have done that, but he was under the control of his dad, Mayor Redburn, who has the dagger that fused him and his spirit beast."

"Why? Why would he do that to Otto?" Everett was now eager to find out more from Marrok.

"He is trying to separate Otto from his spirit beast. We do not think he is acting alone. He shouldn't know the things he does. About the artefact that he needs, how to control Otto and where he needs to open the gateway. Somebody is guiding him, manipulating him from afar." Marrok was clearly genuine with his concern, his body language shifting to reflect this.

"Levent!" Arnold was sure of it, now that it had been broken down, he knew that this had his name all over it. He had been nowhere to be seen throughout everything that had been happening and now suddenly it had turned out he had been manipulating everything from the start.

"We think it is him, yes." Marrok started to withdraw into himself further, like the mere mention of his name caused him to worry.

Arnold felt a new lease of life within him after realising Levent was involved and was eager to learn what he needed to do to help. He would do whatever it took to get to him, more determined than ever to make sure he faced the punishment he deserved for not just his grandad but anyone else that he had ever inflicted pain upon. Arnold had been reignited inside, ready for the fight that was sure to come soon. "What do you need me to do?"

"We have Otto and we will fight to keep him safe. He is well protected with us. We need you to keep the final piece of the puzzle safe, no matter what." Arnold frowned.

"The final piece? What is that then? What am I going to be looking after?"

"Not what Arnold, but who." Marrok turned to face George, who suddenly looked incredibly uncomfortable and began to squirm in the corner of the room where she sat. She stood up looking perplexed at what Marrok was saying as none of it was making any sense.

Everett walked over to George and held her trembling hand to reassure her. "This doesn't make sense. What does George have to do with any of this?"

"Her blood. It's about her blood." Marrok's answer was concise and straight to the point.

Arnold looked back at the confrontations that he had had with the were-jaguar and he kicked himself for not picking up on the link. The first attack was directly on George. The second was right outside the storage container. Both times it was Arnold that had stood against it. Both times he had not been the target, it had been George. The third time they faced off, when Otto transformed in front of their very eyes, Otto was trying to escape them, he was fighting them off desperate to get away. All he wanted was to get his target which must have been the artefact that he had ransacked George's granny's shop for before giving it to Mayor Redburn. The only question that remained was why.

"I presume you are going to tell us the reason that George is so key to this?" Everett asked Marrok, her patience growing thin. She had wrapped her arms around George, who looked terrified, to try and calm her and let her know that she was there for her. Not that this was ever in question; Everett and George had always had each other's backs and that wasn't going to change any time soon. George rested her head against Everett and began to tear up.

"George, I am sorry. It was your Granny, you see. You share her blood and her abilities. You have it in you to be a shaman." George still looked confused.

"But why me? Why our blood? I don't understand?" George continued to tremble, none of this was adding up.

"Your granny was the shaman that opened the gateway to banish Arnold's Grandma. Her spirit is linked to opening a new gateway to bring her back and her energy lives on in you." Marrok picked up the journal that Arnold had been reading and took it across to her. "Read this. It will explain everything. She is mentioned many times. She helped Arnold's grandad and Charles Grey with their work within the Chichen and quite often was the key to their success."

"What about you? Why can't the Almec keep her safe? Surely that's the best place for her if she needs protecting?" Arnold was curious to know why they could protect Otto but not George.

"No!" Marrok raised his voice. "Whatever happens, they cannot be together; that is what he wants, that is what they need to open the gateway. You need to protect her Arnold. You cannot let them take her."

"What are you going to do?" Everett wanted to know.

"I need to report back to the Almec, but if you need me, call me and I will get to you as soon as I can." With that, Marrok headed to exit the storage container. "I'm truly sorry for this burden, George," he said and then disappeared into the courtyard, heading back to the Almec camp.

The three of them sat in silence for a while, each of them trying their hardest to comfort George who was crying her eyes out. She had only just lost her Granny and was still coming to terms with it and now she was in danger. Levent was out there somewhere and he had masterminded all of this. He had been manipulating Mayor Redburn all this time. He had been waiting in the shadows and was still to show his face. He had been there all along and now he needed Otto and George to finalise his plan.

"This isn't fair," George cried into Everett's arms, "Why me? Why does it have to be me?"

Arnold put his arms around Everett and George and

tightly hugged them, not wanting to let either of them go. It was his job to keep her safe and that is what he intended to do. He wouldn't let any harm come to her, not while he was still breathing.

"I'm going to keep you safe George, I promise," Arnold said, trying to reassure her.

"I'm going to hold you to that." Everett squeezed his hand tightly, fully aware of the burden that she had just placed on him..

CHAPTER 21

The sun was especially harsh with the humidity making the air feel sticky, it felt like his body was wrapped skin-tight in clingfilm. He stood with the other two tribesmen momentarily taking in what was due to happen that day. His body was highly decorated and the tribesman had done everything they needed to do to prepare him, in appearance anyway but there was still a long way to go just to settle his nerves.

"Good luck, my friend."

"Not that you will need it."

The two tribesmen patted Levent on the shoulder. "Shall we go?" Levent nodded and took a large breath to try and steady his nerves, but he felt as though he could collapse at any moment. He followed the two tribesmen out of his hut and through the village. As he began to walk the other members of the tribe began to sing and chant as they joined his procession. They continued their journey through a densely wooded area. The crowd grew larger and larger as the whole village was participating in this momentous occasion; the Shaman's daughter was getting married.

Levent felt in a daze as he continued to make his way to the ceremonial stones, concentrating on not tripping over any roots that lay hidden on the ground. He felt sheltered from the sun, but he could feel himself becoming incredibly hot and it showed in the form of sweat beading on his head. He pushed on through the heat and the terrain eager to get to his destination as quickly as possible. He was soon to marry Kaliska and in all truth he just wanted the ceremony to be over and for them both to be man and wife. It was not too long before he could see the ceremonial stones in the distance which were a series of millennia-old ancient blocks that lay on the ground in no particular order. There were five overall, varying in sizes and shapes. The stone monument was a place where the Shaman would come to meditate. He had always told Levent that the area had a great connection to the spirit world and that their tribe had been conducting ceremonies here going back many generations. Now it was the turn of Levent and Kaliska to be married here and Levent could not think of a more beautiful place for it to happen. As they reached the stones, the two tribesmen stepped to the sides and allowed Levent to walk through between them both. Levent obliged and once he made it past them, he could see the Shaman sat atop one of the stones with his legs crossed while he meditated. Levent could hear him humming and chanting to himself as he made his way over to the part of the ceremonial site he had been instructed to when practicing.

Levent watched intently as the Shaman continued his meditation and waited for him to acknowledge his presence. He could feel his legs trembling beneath him and his heart began to beat harder as his time to marry Kaliska drew ever closer. After a few minutes, Levent began to feel uncomfortable at the Shaman not acknowledging him, so he thought he might be best letting him know he was there just in case he didn't realise.

"Any advice before we get started?" He needed to clear his throat before he started as his mouth felt incredibly dry.

"Yes, don't interrupt the Shaman that is blessing your marriage." He opened his eyes and smiled at Levent, who was stood looking incredibly nervous below him. Levent cracked a smile back but could not tell whether the Shaman was joking with him, which in turn made his stomach feel as though it had just been turned inside out. Had he just offended the Shaman right before he was married to his daughter? What if he decided to curse him now rather than bless him or even worse withdraw his consent to them getting married?

"Relax Levent. I am only joking with you." His words were failing to relieve Levent of his worries. "It is not very often a Shaman gets the opportunity to conduct the ceremony of his daughter getting married, allow me that moment to wind you up. You can relax now. You look as though you are ready for a funeral, not your marriage." Levent laughed at the Shaman's words and the knot in his stomach changed from a feeling of worry to one of apprehension. What was taking Kaliska so long? Why was she not here yet?

"She will be here at any moment. You are making me nervous, calm down, my boy."

Levent felt he should do as he was told and tried to steady his nerves. Regulating his breathing, he stood there with his hands behind his back as he awaited Kaliska's arrival. He did not have to wait long before he could hear the soft tone of some of the tribe's women singing as they escorted Kaliska to the ceremonial stones.

Levent's heart fluttered as he anticipated her arrival and as soon as she appeared behind the escorting women, his nerves disappeared in an instant. Her beauty was like none that he had ever seen, her dark skin complemented by the reflecting light from the stones. It was as though her skin was shimmering in the sun. She looked truly radiant and as their eyes met, they cast a smile at one another. Levent caught sight of the enchanting tribal dress that she was wearing and could not help but wonder at the time that the tribeswomen must have put into creating such a mesmerising dress for Kaliska on her wedding day. He knew that Kaliska and her closest friends had been working on this dress for several years in preparation of this day.

Levent stood, wishing to savour this moment. Kaliska looked so beautiful and the smile on her face was the happiest that he had ever seen her. He just wanted her to be stood with him now so they could share this magical moment. He loved her with all his heart. She had saved him when he was at his lowest and his most desperate. He would never forget falling in love with her the first time that he had met her, her kindness like nothing he had ever experienced. She accepted him straight away, accepted his horrific scars, never once being fazed, or becoming afraid by them. She calmed him when he had nightmares about his past and reassured him that everything would be ok. She had given her heart to him and in return, he wanted to provide her with his soul.

He continued to look towards Kaliska, entranced at her smile when he felt an unexpected force against his shoulder which caught him off guard and threw off his balance. He looked towards Kaliska as he began to fall to the floor and her smile turned to horror as she screamed out towards him. He slammed against the floor and a shooting pain went down the entire right side of his body. He looked at his shoulder and saw an arrow protruding out of it. He could hear screams ring out around him as people realised what had just happened, someone had just tried to kill him, but why? His first and only thought at this moment was Kaliska, so he began to bring himself back to his feet but could see nothing but panic all around him. Women and children had started to run to safety as the tribesmen readied themselves to fight and protect them. Levent frantically looked around but he could not see Kaliska anywhere. He looked behind him and saw the Shaman point out towards the trees before he began to roar.

"Chichen!" he bellowed out.

Levent followed the direction he was pointing and could see that some men and women had emerged from the trees. They wore different coloured robes with crests on them. There must have been about twenty of them which was more than double the number of tribesmen.

"Where's Kaliska?" Levent called out to the Shaman. Her safety was his priority and all that he could think about. "Did you see where she went?"

"She was ushered back towards the village for her safety. Are you ok?" The Shaman responded also concerned for Kaliska but also worried that Levent had taken an arrow through his shoulder. The tip of the weapon had exited the back of his shoulder.

Levent grabbed hold of the arrow and snapped it, wincing slightly at the pain. He looked towards the large group before him, looking for who had shot an arrow at him. "Why are they here? Why now?" he questioned, hoping that the Shaman would have the answers.

"They have come for artefacts, like before. They have come for your blade. We will not allow that." He pointed towards the attackers and his entire body began to glow a cyan colour; he was channelling his auro. Before he could do anything, another arrow flew by Levent and buried itself deep within the Shaman's chest, forcing him to leave the floor such was the force that impacted him.

"No!" Levent cried and he pulled out his blade, his anger taking hold of him. It was a rage that he had not felt before, not even when he was tortured in the spirit world by his mother's dragon. Levent could feel a rage building up inside of him and he let out a mighty cry at the anguish and pain caused by seeing someone who had been like a father to him struck down by an arrow. His cry was drowned out by the roar of his lions as they formed at either side of him, they instantly rushed forwards towards the group that had attacked them, taking two of them out immediately.

Realising that the Shaman had been taken down with an arrow, the rest of the tribe let out a battle cry and began to run at the robed men and women who had all started channelling their auros to summon their spirit beasts. A collective rainbow of colours lit up the trees as each of the tribe's people began drawing on their auros in their time of need.

Levent ran towards the Shaman and tried to sit him up, blood was leaving his body at an alarming rate and it was pooling beneath him.

"You need to find Kaliska. You need to save her." His auro began to fade from around him.

"But what about you?" Levent didn't want to leave him but knew that he could not stay if he were to honour his wishes. The Shaman grabbed hold of Levent's hand and began to focus his auro. Levent felt a strange sensation coming over him, the pain in his shoulder dulled and his anger began to clear like a fog being moved by the wind. Everything became clearer to him.

"What are you doing?"

"There is more than one way that I can live. I am channelling my auro to you. This will help you become stronger and to understand. Please, you need to sav Kali.." He closed his eyes as the cyan glow around him began to fade, he slumped into Levent's arms and his body became motionless. His life had faded away, taken for no apparent reason.

Levent could hear the roars, moans, groans and shouting from everyone who was in combat as well as the various spirit animals that had been summoned to fight against each other. None were louder than Levent's lions who he could hear but not see. Levent lowered the Shaman down to the ground and gathering himself. He stood up and ran towards the battle, his fists clenched and his blade outstretched. He needed to get to Kaliska. Two robed people stepped into his path and attempted to block him, but he slammed his fist into one of their chests and they crumpled instantly unable to tolerate the brutal force they had just been met with. He swung his blade out at the other attacker who was not fast enough to block the blow and Levent felt the blade pierce his flesh. He continued his run back towards the village.

He was sprinting as fast as he could. He could hear the trees rustling behind him and glanced over to see that it was his lions that were catching him up, wanting to aid him in finding Kaliska. His feet were battered and bleeding from the rough terrain. Even more blood cascaded down his shoulder like a crimson stream. He was unfazed by this and continued to head to the village, pushing himself through the light-headedness he was currently experiencing through his loss of blood.

He finally reached the village and he desperately tried to spot where Kaliska was. His chest was pounding and his breathing was heavy, his worry unimaginable. He did not know what he would do should anything happen to her.

There was a scream from just beyond Levent's hut, towards the shelter in the middle of the village. Levent made his way across and could see three men from the Chichen stood there in their robes. They had hold of Kaliska as well as some other women from the tribe.

"Kaliska!" Levent called out towards her, wanting her to know that he was here. He did not care for his safety he merely wished for hers. One of the robed men turned towards him and Levent's anger rose even further as he realised who it was stood before him. It was the man that Levent had faced off against twelve years before when he had summoned his lions in front of everyone for the first time. He had a bow hanging over his shoulder and Levent knew instantly that it was he who had shot him in the shoulder and that it was he who had so callously and needlessly killed the Shaman. How was he going to tell Kaliska that her father had been killed and that he had been unable to stop it from happening?

His fury took over and he walked towards the men with his blade in his hand, his intent stare focused purely on the leader of the group. He did not care that he was outnumbered and he didn't need his lions for what he was going to do. He wanted to deal with this himself and there was no way that he would let them get away with what they had done.

"Stop right there," the leader called out. "Come any closer and I am going to have no choice but to kill this pretty little thing. Those lions over there are quite the problem. Let's put them away, eh?" Levent stopped in his tracks. He could see that the leader had one arm tightly around Kaliska with the other holding a blade against her throat. Levent was furious, but he called his lions back towards his blade as he had been commanded to. He didn't want to use them against them anyway. He wanted to savour ending this man's life with his own hands.

"What have you done? I told you to let me handle this!" A man stepped out from within the thick trees of the forest, his robes were torn and his head bloodied. He was most certainly part of the Chichen, although he looked older than the others. "Capture not kill, that is our way. It's our fundamental rule."

"Well, the old man shouldn't have got in the way. I was aiming for him." The leader nodded towards Levent and smiled at him, trying to goad him into a reaction. "This is personal. It's between him and me, Hershel. This does not concern you."

"Please just let her go. I beg you." Levent held his hands up as a peace offering. He just wanted him to let her go.

"She does mean a lot to you, doesn't she?" he teased Levent.

"Let her go." The robed man commanded. The man holding Kaliska didn't move. "I am your Elder, now let her go!" The man smirked and pushed Kaliska forward. Levent's relief was short-lived as the man quickly drew his bow and launched an arrow into her back. Her face looked shocked as the arrow burst into her and she let out a whimper as she began to fall.

"No!" Levent roared as his rage consumed him. Why had he done this? Why would he fire an arrow into a defenceless woman? It was cowardice at its worst. Without hesitating Levent launched his dagger through the air, but the man pulled one of the other robed men into his path, they took the full force of the blade as it embedded in his chest. His breathing gurgled as he drew his last breath. The man grinned at Levent as he set off into the woods. Levent wanted to give chase but heard Kaliska call out for him.

"Levent!" The sound of his love struggling to breathe cut him deeper than any weapon could. He couldn't bear to lose her and could not believe what had happened. This was supposed to be their big day. They had wanted this for so long. His entire existence was down to her, she made him feel whole. She had made him feel human again.

The robed man had summoned his spirit beast and a large Elk stood over Kaliska trying to ease her pain as she lay wounded on the floor. "Please let me try and heal her. I can help." He placed his hands out and began to use his auro to ease her suffering further.

Levent felt a twinge inside his brain, like a rubber band snapping. "Stay away from her!" He ran towards the body on the floor and removed his blade from his chest. He was beyond angry. "I said, get off her!" The man looked so sorrowful.

"Please, she is dying and she needs my help." Levent's anger was rising to a new level and he could feel his auro coursing through his body like electricity. He had never felt power like it and he wanted to use it to punish everyone from the Chichen. He could feel his auro surging as the orange energy from his blade engulfed his entire body. Behind him, he noticed something; something that he had not seen for a long time. An area just before the trees to the side of the shelter became distorted. He recognised it straight away as a gateway, a portal to the spirit world which he had travelled through so many years ago and had not seen since.

He could feel a pull towards the portal, like a magnet and he knew what was happening. It was drawing him in and he had no control over it. "No! I can't! Kaliska!" He was fighting against the pull as hard as he could. It was too late and he was dragged through the distorted gateway, screaming as he tried to fight against it. His efforts were pointless. The last thing he could see before being pulled through was the robed man knelt over Kaliska who lay on the floor motionless, her life drifting away from her.

He was back in the spirit world, he knew straight away as the air he was breathing felt different. There was no breeze, no heat burning down from above like in his village. He crawled around frantically on the floor where he had landed, hoping that he would go back through the distorted portal that had pulled him back to this place, but it had vanished. His frustration manifested in a scream of anguish. He had just seen the Shaman die in his arms, his auro now a part of him. Levent didn't know how to process his grief. Worse still, he had just seen his sweet Kaliska gravely wounded having taken an arrow in her back, the man from the Chichen trying his hardest to heal her despite it being one of his colleagues that had shot the arrow into her. He had many emotions all at once; anger, frustration, sadness, despair. Why take their lives when it could have been him?

"It should have been me!" His tears were beginning to stream down his face and dampen the dry floor where he knelt. He began to punch the floor in frustration, a way of venting his anger. Levent pounded the ground over and over until his hands began to bleed. he gritted his teeth tightly, his face distorted with rage and fury. He needed to find a way back. He needed to get back to his tribe to help Kaliska, but the problem was he had no idea how he was going to get back. The few times he had transported had been sporadic and he had no control or understanding of why these portals opened for him. The portal that had so cruelly torn him away from Kaliska when she needed him the most was the first one he had seen in twelve years. Levent continued to scream into the air as he knew that there was nothing he could do to save Kaliska. The desperation and frustration he felt gave him physical and almost unbearable pain, consuming every part of him until there was nothing left but pure anger.

He needed to get back, he wanted to make everyone pay for taking everything away from him. He wanted revenge against anyone who had ever hurt him. His mum, the dragon that was tethered to her, whoever was responsible for killing his sweet Kaliska and the Shaman.
Levent let out a roar of anguish, he was not going to stop until he had his revenge.

CHAPTER 22

Arnold didn't know what to do. For the first time ever he felt he could not turn to his dad for help or advice on his current situation and it was killing him.

George and Arnold remained holed up at the storage container, not knowing what to do. George looked increasingly pensive about the plan, the weight of the situation taking its toll on her. Everett had left the container to get some supplies for them from the shop. She said she was going to get dressed too but she had been gone longer than expected. The two of them had started to worry that she might have been taken until Everett calmly appeared at the door with a carrier bag full of sandwiches, crisps and drinks. She seemed completely oblivious as to why they were both looking at her with their eyebrows raised.

"Took your time much? We were worried, Everett." George stood with her arms folded, less than impressed that she had chosen to take her time getting what they needed given the current situation.

"What? I decided to grab a shower while I was home. You're ok - Arnold is with you." She didn't understand the telling off from George.

"You do pick your moments," Arnold joked, trying to make light of the situation.

They had been at the storage container all morning pacing around and trying to come up with a plan of how to keep George safe. So far, they had managed to come up with nothing. They tucked into their sandwiches quietly while each of them tried to think of what to do next. Arnold couldn't turn to the Chichen, they would discover all of his grandad's belongings which he had accumulated over the years. They would find out that he had been hiding them and they would surely figure out that he was somehow associated with the Almec who actively worked against the Chichen. What was worse, if they found out about his grandad's association with the Almec as well as his collection, the Chichen would call him a traitor and remove the carving in the steps of their station to honour his sacrifice and dedication to them.

Arnold could not understand why his grandad had been working against the Chichen and this was causing Arnold great internal conflict. He couldn't discuss this with his dad for fear of how he would respond and he desperately wanted to protect his grandad's good name. For now, Arnold had no reason to disbelieve the information that they had been given as it correlated with what Arnold had figured out for himself. The Almec had Otto and George was with him. Mayor Redburn had the artefact that he needed but not Otto or George and Arnold needed to ensure that it stayed that way.

"We can't stay in here forever guys. It's not practical," Everett pointed out. She was becoming bored of being holed up in one place.

"That's easy for you to say, it's not you who he is coming after," George fired back.

"Come on, you two. There's no need to fall out." Arnold, tried to play peacekeeper. "I do think we need to come up with another plan other than stopping here. We are sitting ducks."

"Well, it's the best idea, in my opinion," said George.

"What else can we do, if we stay here we might as well just hand her over to Mayor Redburn."

Arnold thought about what Everett had said for a moment. "Actually, that might not be such a bad idea?"

"What?" George said, visibly starting to panic. "What a stupid idea!"

"Hear me out, George." Arnold could understand her initial reluctance. "What if we let him take you?" George and Everett were in a combined state of disbelief at Arnold's words.

"I think you have taken one too many blows to the head." It was safe to say that George opposed Arnold's hair-brained idea. She did not like the idea one bit.

"Let's face it, there is no-one we can go to for help with this. The Chichen might be involved as I've seen Mr. Whittaker speaking with Mayor Redburn about opening the coal mines. What if we allowed you to be taken? I can follow and let Everett know where you are and she can let Marrok know. If they bring the Almec we could stop Mayor Redburn before anything happened." He knew it was a stretch, but what else could they do? They couldn't hide forever.

"Absolutely not! No way Arnold, we will get ourselves killed," George protested, clearly not on board with the idea at all.

"The other option is we wait around looking over our shoulder until he appears or sends someone else to get you."

"I hate to say it George, but I think Arnold has a point. Mayor Redburn would not be expecting Arnold to be so bold and technically he does need Otto too for his plan to work." George stared open-mouthed at them both.

"Seriously you two? What if it goes wrong?"

"Would you rather be looking over your shoulder or would you rather we try and catch him off guard, get the upper hand and capture him?" Arnold was sure that the plan would work; they just needed to find somewhere away from the lock-up. George still did not look impressed, but she looked like she was beginning to give his wild idea a second thought rather than dismissing it outright.

"Why don't we tell Marrok the plan?"

Everett didn't like the idea but understood Arnold's rationale for it. "Because they wouldn't want us to do it. I think this is the best way. We follow you and we catch him."

"What could possibly go wrong?" George's sarcasm was emitting from every inch of her body language. "So where are we going to hatch this plan, then?" Everett shrugged.

"Where do teenagers hang around at the weekend? It's certainly not old dusty storage containers." Arnold couldn't answer as his weekends had been spent training at the Chichen and more recently here. Arnold and George both looked at Everett waiting for her to tell them where they would put George as bait.

"The nature reserve at Fox hill bank," she suggested.

Arnold agreed that this was a good idea with its location away from the general population. Hopefully, this would help to prevent anyone else from getting hurt. The nature reserve sat just outside the centre of town and was a short walk from where they were. All they needed to do was draw Mayor Redburn out by making sure they walked down all the main roads on their way there and hoped that he would see them.

"Right it's decided then," Arnold confirmed with both of them nodding in agreement. George looked more nervous than ever. "I won't let anything happen to you, George. I promise." The three of them readied themselves to leave.

"You'd better not." George quipped.

Arnold grabbed his macuahuitl and placed its harness over his head. He shut the container and held his hand against the elk hieroglyph that decorated the side and waited for the locks to kick in. The three of them left the lock up and began their journey towards Foxhill nature reserve, their dangerous plan now set in motion. They all knew there was a lot that could go wrong, but it was the only chance to catch Mayor Redburn and stop anything really bad from happening.

They continued through the streets of Oswald. The roads seemed eerily quiet as though the town knew of the showdown that would ensue should their plan work. They made their way across the overgrown field that sat in front of the nature reserve and disappeared into the trees. They escorted George down the path towards the central bank which was filled with water. Locals did visit here from time to time to walk their dogs or come and feed the ducks but it was quiet today. Once they got to the bank, they readied themselves to leave George.

Everett wrapped her arms around her and gave her a massive hug. George and Everett were so close and as the two of them remained in their hug with Everett became tearful.

"We will be right over there." Arnold pointed to some trees that were surrounded by bushes and shrubs to keep their location hidden. "If anything goes wrong, I will be out straight away."

"You'd better be," George said before hugging Arnold.

Everett and Arnold headed to their hiding point and removed themselves from sight. They sat on the floor next to each other, waiting awkwardly like. Hours passed and they remained at the nature reserve waiting for Mayor Redburn to make a move against them. It was surely just a matter of time. Boredom had well and truly set in with the three of them waiting in silence.

Arnold's phone vibrated in his pocket. He removed it to see who was ringing and saw that it was Marrok.

"Hello," he whispered, not wanting to draw attention to Everett and himself who remained under cover of the trees and bushes.

"Arnold. It's Otto. He's got out."

"What do you mean got out? How does that even

happen? There's quite a few of you there," Arnold hissed. He couldn't believe they had managed to lose Otto.

"He is stronger than we anticipated! He hasn't shifted into Night-Sun and he was able to get past us. He is not in control." Arnold knew what Marrok meant by this and realised that their plan must have worked. Mayor Redburn had taken the bait and regained control of Otto through the use of the blade he was linked to. He looked up and saw someone heading down the path towards George. "I'll call you back, Marrok." Arnold hung up on him and used his enhanced vision to focus on the figure that was heading through the nature reserve. It was Otto but his eyes looked considerably paler than usual. It was the vacant expression that Arnold had become accustomed to Otto having when he was under the control of his dad. Otto's pace was quick and as he drew closer. George spotted him and Arnold could see the panic on her face.

Everett went to stand up but Arnold grabbed her arm and pulled her back down towards him.

"We can't let those two be together, that's what Marrok said." She spoke with conviction, desperately wanting to help her best friend.

"I know, but if we intervene now, we won't get another chance to find Mayor Redburn. This is our best chance of catching him and ending this."

Otto grabbed hold of George's arm who tried to pull against him, but he was far stronger than she and so she reluctantly gave in and began to follow him as they exited the nature reserve together.

"Ring Marrok, find him. I will follow and let you know where we end up." Arnold stood up and began to follow the two of them out of the nature reserve and up through town. They continued to walk at a fast pace and Arnold was trying his hardest to remain out of sight. They walked past a derelict factory which used to be an old chemical plant, through the overgrown grounds and across the field behind. Continuing his pursuit, Arnold was able to easily keep them insight with the help of his enhanced vision.

Once across the field the two of them appeared to disappear with Arnold instantly recognising the location. It was where the entrance to the coal mine was; Otto had taken George straight there. Arnold sped up his pursuit when the two of them disappeared. He pulled his phone out and began to type out a text and sent it to Everett to tell them where they were.

With Otto and George now together, their initial plan had changed. Arnold knew that he could no longer wait for the backup to arrive in the form of the Almec as they had initially agreed. He needed to get inside and prevent any harm happening to George as he still didn't know how Mayor Redburn planned to use both her and Otto. He reached the entrance to the mine and saw that the usually flooded entrance had been drained. The large machine that had done this was still switched on, the noise sounded like a chugging car engine.

Arnold wanted to end this. He wanted to save his friends. He just hoped that his training had paid off and he was strong enough to do it.

CHAPTER 23

Arnold stood at the entrance to the cave, his senses heightened. He needed to stop Mayor Redburn from opening a portal to the spirit world no matter what. It was dusk and the birds were now settling into their nests for the night. There was a slight breeze in the air and Arnold took a large gulp of breath, knowing that once inside the tunnel there was only going to be stale air until he resurfaced.

He stepped into the muddied entrance, recently unearthed after decades of being submerged underwater. He trudged his way through the thick sludge until he came to a door. Grabbing hold of a copper-coloured rusted handle, Arnold pulled the door open with so much force, he nearly pulled the whole thing off its decrepit hinges. Arnold dreaded seeing what it was like inside if this was the condition on the outside. Knowing it was only going to get worse but desperate to save his friends, he decided to bite the bullet and step forwards into the pitch-black tunnel.

Arnold concentrated and illuminated a slight glow before his eagle manifested in front of him. The light it emitted gave light to the immediate area meaning Arnold could now see down the winding mine tunnels for a short distance. The tunnel was narrow, meaning his eagle could not fly. A slight splatting noise could be heard from its feet skipping through the bog-like floor next to Arnold. Arnold continued to concentrate, trying to use his enhanced vision, but with the darkness ahead, it was hard to see clearly. He needed to keep a calm and cool head so he could think rationally when he confronted Mayor Redburn.

He continued through the tunnel slowly, trying to make as little noise as possible. The further he descended, the thinner the air seemed to get, a stale taste lingering in his mouth from the musty air that he was breathing in. He moved down the narrow tunnel for some time before, he could see that further ahead of him was illuminated. He could hear voices faintly echoing up towards him, which gradually became clearer as he approached.

"Let me go!" George cried.

"If you don't start talking, I will have to bind your mouth again," Mayor Redburn barked back. Arnold lifted his hand to the hilt of his macahuitl and kept it firmly in his grasp, prepared to draw his weapon at any time to save George and Otto. Arnold drew level to the chamber where they were and knelt behind a rock so that he could survey the area and devise a plan of action. Gazing over the uneven surface of the dirt-covered rock, he glanced around the room to see where everyone was standing. George was tied up next to what looked like a mine shaft that would go even further down below. Otto stood next to her with a vacant expression on his face. Opposite the two of them with his back turned to them was Mayor Redburn. He was wearing what looked like armour, the patterned skin of a tiger lined his tunic which Arnold presumed was his spirit animal knowing that Otto's family all shared spirit animals of the big cat variety. He had a weapon strapped to his back which Arnold focused on a little more to figure out what it was. After a moment of studying, he realised that it was a morning star; a short wooden handle was attached to a chain with a solid metal ball on the end of it, with more spikes protruding from it than Arnold dared to count.

Mayor Redburn was much older than him and he had many years of training under his belt. Mayor Redburn had his hands outstretched and appeared to be holding a chalice in one of them. He continued to move around the room, waving the chalice around in the air until he abruptly stopped.

"It's here, this point. This is it." His hands began to glow, the flow of the energy generating a powerful force around him. "It's directly below us, this is the point, can you feel the energy? Get ready to take her down," he commanded. Otto grabbed hold of George's arm and began to walk towards his dad like he had been instructed. He looked emotionless like he wasn't even there.

"Get off me, Otto!" George barked. "What are you doing?!" She attempted to dig her feet into the ground, but Otto was much stronger than her and attempting to stop him was futile.

Mayor Redburn started chanting. "We are done here, bring her down the mine shaft. Then we can summon the portal."

Sensing this was his moment to step in. Arnold stepped out from behind the rock and pulled his macuahuitl from its holster on his back. He took a stance with both his hands gripped around the hilt of his ancient weapon. "Let her go," he growled, not knowing if this was aimed at Mayor Redburn or Otto.

"Ethon," Mayor Redburn hissed, "You just keep getting in the way, don't you? I have to do this. It's the only way."

"I know you are summoning a portal and I know it is for her. I'm not going to let that happen." His eyes did not shift from Mayor Redburn, not wanting to show any sign of intimidation. "Let George go. You don't need her." Mayor Redburn began laughing

"But I do Ethon, I do. She is the key." Arnold frowned. "What are you on about?"

"To the portal, she is a shaman! Like her grandmother was. She was the shaman that helped trap your grandma in the spirit world. Her essence is in the girl and I need to extract that essence to release her."

"I've already told you, I am not going to let that happen." He took a step forward, but his path was blocked by Otto who had let go of George and turned to face him.

"I didn't want to have to do this, but I have no choice," the Mayor said.

"You chose to do this to Otto, your son. How could you do this to him?" Arnold roared.

"If it wasn't me, it would be someone else. That's why I keep the dagger. I need to open that portal so I can release him from his spirit beast." Arnold shook his head.

"And turn him into menial! Have you ever asked him what he wants?"

Otto dropped to his knees and began to contort; he was shifting into his were-jaguar form. The cracking noise of his bones breaking into shape was causing Otto great pain and he winced and groaned as his body changed before him. A green glow emitted from him and within a few moments, he had turned into the were-jaguar. He stood up tall and let out a low-pitched grumble as he stared down Arnold, that wild and feral look taking over his eyes. He did not move. he just stood blocking Arnold's path to George. Arnold thought back to the last time they had gone toe to toe and Otto had thrown him around the lock-up like a rag doll. This time however he had his weapon and George's safety depended on him.

"Take care of him and meet me in the pit," Mayor Redburn ordered and he began to walk towards the mine shaft, gripping George's arm and dragging her along with him.

"Let me go!" She cried once more.

Arnold stepped forward but Otto swung a razorsharp, claw at him. Arnold quickly brought his macuahuitl upwards to shield himself from the blow. Otto spun and swung his other hand around with Arnold knocking this away. Otto continued with this process multiple times swinging his claws wildly at Arnold, relentlessly trying to shred him. Arnold parried each blow while stepping back each time, meaning that Otto was gaining more and more momentum as the two of them began their duel. The battle even harder for Arnold, as he did not wish to hurt Otto, however he was not in control and had been instructed to stop Arnold.

Otto raised a hand in the air and swung wildly at Arnold once more, Arnold ducked underneath the attack. Arnold turned his macuahuitl on its side and smacked the flat side of the panel against the side of the were-jaguar with as much force as he could muster. Sending him face-first into the wall beside them. Arnold jumped away to make some distance between the two of them, but the beast had pushed itself from the wall and thrown itself at Arnold. Diving at Arnold with his mouth wide open, it attempted to lock its brutal jaws around him. Arnold grabbed hold of the top of his macuahuitl and turned it sideways to shield himself, the were-jaguar's jaws wrapped around it. Arnold rolled backwards and lifted his feet into its chest and kicked it over the top of him before quickly jumping back to his feet so that he could continue to defend himself.

Otto continued to growl ferociously and began to pace around Arnold, stalking his prey. Arnold's eagle flew out from behind the rock into the open space. Sinking its talons into Otto's side it attempted to lift him again. Otto had got wise to this move though and grabbed hold of it with both hands, biting down onto one of its wings. The eagle let out a shrill shriek as Otto began shaking its head violently as it attempted to detach its wing from its body. Panicking, Arnold rushed at it and swung his macuahuitl against the back of its head, making the beast let go of its prey. It spun and hurled the injured eagle through the air, straight at Arnold smashing him in the chest and knocking him to the ground.

Arnold gasped, attempting to regain his breath from the blow, the force taking him by surprise. His eagle lay injured so Arnold focused his auro and it began to dissipate within him protecting it from any further harm. His shoulder was throbbing intensely from the pain his eagle had experience with that last blow.

The room was too open for Arnold to get the upper hand against Otto so he glanced around the room looking for any kind of opening. He could see a darkened tunnel just past the mine shaft where Mayor Redburn had taken George. Despite its darkness, Arnold made a run for it, setting off at pace to get as close to them as he could in a short space of time. Otto immediately gave chase, snapping ferociously at Arnold's heels. Arnold could hear him right behind him and entered the darkness, unable to see the bends and curves of the mine until the very last moment. The beast right behind him was baying for Arnold's blood and he put everything he had into keeping the minuscule gap between them. The tunnel walls were flying past him and Arnold continued to dodge rocks and posts, some a little too close for comfort. Arnold was running off instinct now and was amazed that he had not clattered into anything. Ahead of him, he saw a post. He swung his macuahuitl into it. The post splintered in half, dropping in front of Otto and giving Arnold that split second extra as Otto smashed through the debris before him. In front of Arnold was a dead-end that he was fast approaching. He was out of space and out of ideas and he needed to act quickly. Using a large rock in front of him he used it to propel himself at the wall, outstretching his legs he then pushed back against the wall and catapulted himself back at the pursuing beast which had also thrown itself through the air with its claws outstretched. This was Arnold's last chance. It was a matter of survival and he slammed the side of his macahuitl with incredible force, giving it everything he had into the side of Otto's head and sending him hurtling back to the ground. Otto's head bounced off the rock and he slid to a stop as he reached the wall. Arnold ground to a halt as he skimmed across the floor like a thin stone projecting across a lake. He rolled repeatedly and came to a stop and let out a laboured groan as he pushed himself up from the floor. He stood momentarily with his stare planted on the feral beast that lay motionless on the floor; after a moment he could see that it was breathing. The beast was unconscious, Arnold had won and they were both alive. Arnold turned and set off running back towards the mine shaft. He was exhausted from that confrontation, but he knew there was more to come. He needed to stop Mayor Redburn and to save George.

CHAPTER 24

The taste of iron engulfed Arnold's throat, his shoulder was red hot with pain and he was covered in cuts and grazes. The ache in Arnold's body was tremendous, but George's situation was what was keeping him going at this moment. He needed to get to her no matter what and as soon as possible. He made it to the mine shaft where they had travelled down. Not wanting to draw attention to himself, he made the decision that he needed to climb down rather than calling the lift up to him.

He placed his macuahuitl back within its holster and grabbed hold of the side of the lift before lowering himself slowly onto one of the beams that were planted within the wall. He then dropped down to the next section, grabbing hold of the next beam and continued this process until he was on top of the of the elevator. He opened the hatch and slid through as delicately as he could without making any excess noise. The gate to the elevator was already pulled to one side so Arnold exited before carrying on down the darkened tunnel. The air felt at its thinnest here and despite not being claustrophobic, he certainly understood how those who suffered from the condition felt. The tunnel was incredibly narrow compared to the ones that were above. Arnold could feel the ground beneath him was sloped and the tunnel was spiralling as if on an ancient staircase. He reached the bottom where he could see a faint glow growing brighter as he edged ever lower beneath the surface. Arnold reached a door opening and crept through slowly. He could see George tied up in the centre of the room. She made eye contact with him and tried to shout towards him, but her mouth was gagged. All that Arnold could hear were her muffled cries. Her eyes grew large, Arnold knew it was too late. He felt a blow to his head and then everything went dark.

When he came to, he found his hands had been bound. They were tied behind him around some chains that were bolted to the floor. He attempted to pull away, but the bindings were fastened tightly around his wrists, making it almost impossible to move. Arnold looked around the room and could see Mayor Redburn stood with George by his side. She was still trying her hardest to pull away from him, but her attempts did not get her anywhere.

"Arnold! Are you ok?" she asked.

"Never better." A dull throbbing pain engulfed the side of his face where he had been knocked unconscious. He had no idea how long he had been out.

"Quiet!" Mayor Redburn commanded. The air became distorted, as though looking through frosted glass. Arnold knew what was happening, he recognised the distortion from the tower the night his grandad was murdered. The portal was there for them all to see and after a brief moment, a powerfully built man stepped through the portal and stood face to face with Mayor Redburn. His large black overcoat moving with the energy that was emitting from the distortion behind him. His heavily scarred face was recognisable straight away as he stood tall with a crooked smile. Showing his delight at the current situation.

Arnold felt his rage build inside him. It was Levent. The

monster who had turned his life upside down, the person who had kidnapped him, taunted him, goading him to summon his spirit beast so that he could steal it for himself. Arnold had known deep down that Levent would show his horrifically disfigured face again. He could not believe that Mayor Redburn had been working with him this entire time. Arnold tried to pull his hands free so that he could show them both exactly what he thought of them. His efforts were pointless with his bindings still tightly restraining him. All the hatred he had for Levent came rushing back and he could feel his body trembling with pure rage.

"Do you have it?" Levent's rasping voice echoed around the mine.

"Here." Mayor Redburn passed him the chalice that was in his hand. Levent took it from Mayor Redburn and he began checking over the chalice.

"I presume this is the girl?" he said, nodding in George's direction.

"Yes, she is the granddaughter of the shaman who helped trap your mother in the spirit world. She has also shown herself to have similar abilities."

"Let me go!" George started pulling away from Mayor Redburn, unable to look Levent in the eyes, his face was the stuff of nightmares. Levent lashed out and smacked George across the face, the backhanded slap busting George's lip. If not for being gripped by Mayor Redburn, George would have been launched across the room such was the force that he used against her. Arnold felt powerless and another wave of fury erupted from within; how could he hit someone so much weaker than him and so hard?

"Get off her!" he screamed, "I'll kill you! I'll kill both of you for this!"

Levent looked over the shoulder of Mayor Redburn and grinned at Arnold. "Sit tightly, boy. I'm sure you will have your chance soon enough," his gruff voice goading Arnold. Levent pulled out his blade from within his jacket and grabbed hold of George's arm pulling it out towards him.

George continued to struggle and shrieked as Levent drew the blade across her arm, turning it crimson instantly. George let out a shrill scream from the pain as Levent squeezed her forearm tightly, causing her blood to come gushing out of the open wound. He placed the chalice underneath and collected her blood. Levent then placed the chalice on the floor and used the same blade to cut his hand before clenching his fist and dripping his blood into the chalice as well. "I share the blood of the dragon trapped within the spirit world. You share the blood of the shaman that trapped her there." He looked around the room as though trying to spot something. "Where is he?"

Arnold knew straight away that he meant Otto and felt happy, he had slowed the process was, down. He smirked at his small victory, but it was short-lived, no sooner had Levent spoken Otto had appeared at the entrance to the cavern. He had changed back and his head was bleeding heavily from the side, his face swollen.

"All we need now is for him to drink this and he will be parted with his spirit beast. The sacrifice of his spirit beast combined with the consumption of our blood will be enough to create a gateway with enough strength to pull her back into this world." Otto began to stagger forward towards Levent, creating a scuffing noise against the ground as he dragged himself forwards in a zombie-like fashion.

Levent's eyes were open wide with anticipation at what was about to happen and he offered the blood for Otto to drink.

"And when he does this, he will be back to normal? He won't change anymore?" Mayor Redburn interrupted something that Levent seemed far from happy about.

"Seeing as he would no longer have his spirit beast, I would assume so." Levent hissed.

"Assume?"

"Are you questioning me?" Levent was less than impressed at Mayor Redburn's lack of faith in him. He looked angry that the question had been asked.

"No, not at all," he muttered.

Glancing down at the floor Levent noticed Arnold's macuahuitl cast to one side. A smile coming to his sunken, dark eyes. "You have become careless. Leaving your grandad's things lying around like that? This was his weapon of choice, was it not?" Arnold didn't answer, choosing to simply stare him down, not wanting to show any signs that he was intimidated.

"What about the chalice?" Mayor Redburn pressed, wanting for the ritual to start sooner rather than later. Levent sneered at him.

"Ask me again and I will remove your tongue. Now hold this." Levent passed the chalice to Mayor Redburn to hold and walked over to the macuahuitl that lay on the ground just ahead of where Arnold was restrained. Levent picked up the blade with one hand and began to look at the detail of the carvings as though admiring the craft that had gone into it. He began to swing it around in the air, forwards and backwards, as he figured out the weight of the weapon. He moved it with ease, much more so than Arnold could, needing only one hand to be able to wield it whereas Arnold needed to use both of his. "It is a thing of beauty, isn't it?" Levent teased.

"Put it down. You don't deserve to hold it. You are a coward!" Levent smiled, unphased by Arnold's words. He was toying with him, like a lion playing with its food. After continuing to wield the sword for a few minutes, he shrugged before walking over to one of the many large rocks within the chamber and rested it against it. The hilt was balancing against the top of the rock leaving the weapon at a diagonal angle. Levent then began to walk away.

"Now, where were we?" he grinned. "Shall we continue?" He started walking back towards Mayor Redburn, who was still stood next to George and Otto holding the blood-filled chalice. Levent stopped for a moment as if thinking about something carefully before staring Arnold dead in the eye. Spinning on his heels, he ran back towards the weapon and jumped into the air. He landed on the side of the macahuitl, the force of which snapped the blade from the hilt.

"Oops," he said, laughing.

"No!" Arnold was furious he had just destroyed his grandad's weapon. He had put so many hours into practicing with so that one day he could face Levent and beat him to honour his grandad. Levent's laugh echoed around the chamber. He did not care for the pain he had caused Arnold; he thrived on being able to tease him. He took the chalice from Mayor Redburn and began to hum and chant quietly under his breath. The ancient artefact began to glow illuminating Levent's hideous face in a strange green light.

"Open her mouth," he commanded.

"I'm not drinking that!" George cried. Mayor Redburn kicked her in the back of the knees, dropping her to the floor. He pulled her hair back and grabbed her jaw, holding it open. Levent stepped forward and tilted the chalice slightly, allowing the blood within to drip into her mouth and down her neck. Mayor Redburn then pulled her jaw up and held his hand firmly over her mouth until she had no choice but to swallow the contents. After letting go of her George dropped onto all fours trying to spit out what she could, but she was too late; she had swallowed the blood. She began to glow yellow through her Auro.

"I feel funny," George said, panic etched into her face. Her fox spirit beast appeared in front of her, but it was a strange green colour that matched the glow from the chalice. Levent reached forward and grabbed hold of the fox, throwing it behind him towards a distorted gateway that had appeared. The fox's trajectory changed as a purple blur clattered into it, knocking it away from the portal.

"George!" Everett cried, having made her way down the mine shafts. "Leave her alone!" Her boar nuzzled into George's fox before standing in front of it to protect it from Levent.

"The gateway is opening. We just need to feed it enough energy so it can sustain her passing through it," Levent grinned. "Do not be fooled into thinking I need her beast specifically. It was just her blood I needed to start the process." Levent charged at the boar which began to run towards him. He stepped to the side of it and grabbed hold of one of its tusks, pulling it upwards. Levent then used his weight, strength and momentum to thrust the boar towards the portal. Everett's boar let out a shrill shriek until it hit the portal and disappeared, the echoed noise of its cry for help slowly vanishing. Everett dropped to her knees, her eyes wide. Her purple auro faded from around her and tears began to form in her face.

"No!" Arnold cried in harmony with George. His heart was breaking for her. Everett had just had her spirit beast ripped away from her and tossed to one side like it was nothing. Its energy had been absorbed by the gateway and it would never be seen again. She had been turned into a menial, someone without any spirit world energy and without a spirit beast. George looked up at Levent, tears streaming down her face and her body curled up on the floor in agony. "Why would you? Is she-?"

"Gone? Yes, don't worry though. All that energy is being put to good use." He then looked across and passed the chalice to Otto who took hold of the artefact, grasping it with both of his hands awaiting instruction. "Once you drink this, I will use my blade to draw out the spirit beast within you. We will use the combined energy of yours and the other spirit beast to open a gateway strong enough to let her pass through to this side."

Mayor Redburn stared at the chalice in Otto's hands before placing his hand on his dagger and commanding him, "Drink from the chalice, Otto. Drink and we can end this. He can free you." Otto slowly began to raise the chalice to his mouth when Arnold heard something in the background. A noise echoing down the tunnel that led to the chamber. It was growing louder as it drew closer and after a moment Arnold realised what it was.

An orange glow could be seen and a loud howl echoed into the chamber followed by Marrok's white wolf. It sprinted into the room and jumped onto Otto, sending the chalice flying out of his hand and onto the floor. The ground stained red as the mixed blood curdled with the dirt and soil from the earth.

"What!" Levent roared, his anger there for all to see. "Who is this?" Marrok entered the room wearing armour that resembled chainmail. But it did not look metallic; more like it was made from bone. His shoulder pauldrons were spiked and it looked as though he was wearing some form of a cape. This led up to a hood which was the pelt from a wolf. Marrok's amber eyes focused on Levent from underneath.

"The Almec!" Levent roared, his fury taking over. Arnold was confused. Did Levent just say the Almec? How would Levent know Marrok was part of the Almec? "Night-Sun, I am here for Night-Sun," Marrok declared, his stare still firmly planted on Levent. His white wolf had bounded around the room before standing next to him, the light-emitting from it reflecting off his bone armour. "You bring dishonour in trying to destroy Night-Sun. I won't let that happen. You will be punished. The council wills it."

"Your council has no laws that bind me. not any more!" he hissed in response. "They send a pup into a lion's den." With this, Levent summoned his giant mane-less lion with the power from his own blade. The beast let out an ear-splitting roar as it ran towards Marrok. It was bearing its teeth and going straight in for the kill. Marrok's white wolf jumped across and knocked the lion. Marrok was able to dive out of the way before the lion's paw could make contact with his head.

Mayor Redburn made a run for it, leaving George lying on the floor. George immediately made a rush for Everett who lay on the ground near her. Everett had gone into shock from the trauma of being torn away from her spirit beast. Everett wasn't quite done yet and kicked her leg out, hooking it around Mayor Redburn's shin. He lost his balance and slammed down onto the floor, dropping the dagger in the process.

"You coward!" Everett screamed picking up the dagger that had slid in front of her.

Arnold realised that Everett now could control Otto.

"Everett! You need to command Otto! You have the dagger so he will listen to you." Everett looked down at the dagger before switching her line of sight back to Otto. He was fixed to the spot while the lion and white wolf continued to maul each other. The lion's far superior size meant it had the upper hand against its foe. Levent had made a move for Marrok and the two of them had begun combat with Marrok throwing punches and kicks at Levent. He repeatedly dodged these before brutally punching Marrok to the floor, jumping on top of him and starting to rain down blows from above. Marrok raised his arms above his head to protect himself.

"Everett!" his muffled voice called "You must get Otto out of here! You have to keep Night-Sun safe!" Everett couldn't leave Marrok in this position so she gripped the dagger and held it close to her chest.

"Otto you have to listen to me. We need you back - you need to save Marrok. You have to help him!"

Levent broke through Marrok's defence, his relentless onslaught continuing to rain down blows on his head and chest. Otto suddenly snapped back into the room, his vacant look leaving him and he immediately ran towards Marrok. While running, he began to change form once more and as he dived through the air, he completed the transition into Night-Sun. He grabbed hold of Levent and threw him of Marrok while growling ferociously at him. Everett ran across to Arnold and used the dagger to cut through his bindings and release him.

"You need to get Marrok out of here," Arnold explained, "He's badly injured." Everett nodded and ran across the chamber towards Marrok only to be intercepted by Levent's monstrous spirit beast. It roared at Everett who for a moment, felt like her time was up. That was until Otto dived on the back of the lion and pierced its skin with his claws. He then jumped from the lion and landed in front of Everett. Now that he had the full attention of the lion, Everett ran around to help Marrok back to his feet. George sprinted over to help.

"Come on guys!" George placed her hand out to help Marrok up, her fox standing guard and offering some protection. "Come on, Marrok get up." She knelt down and helped Marrok up with Everett before the three of them began to make their way towards the tunnel.

Looking across the room, Arnold could see that Levent was back on his feet and moving towards his friends. He set off running across the chamber towards him, wanting to get to him before he got to George, Everett and Marrok.

"Get out you three!" He yelled. "Quickly!" He jumped across and planted a dropkick on Levent, knocking him to the ground as Arnold ricochet off the floor. He looked across to see George and Everett helping Marrok into the tunnel. He could see Everett clutching Otto's dagger, the soft green glow illuminating the darkness in front of her.

Behind him, Otto and the lion were taking it in turns to maul each other with their claws before Otto managed to grab hold and pin the lions two front legs. The two of them roared at one another, the noise made Arnold's heart beat even harder than it already was. The sound was like nothing he had ever heard before and it shook him to his core.

Arnold climbed back to his feet at the same time as Levent and the two stood facing each other. Levent looked as furious as ever, Arnold stood opposite with both fists tightly clenched, equally angry at everything that Levent had done. He stood for a moment preparing himself for the fight that he was about to have.

"You think you can fight me. You think you are strong enough to kill me. You have no idea!" Levent barked.

"I'm not going to kill you." Arnold ran at Levent again and began with a quick one-two punch combination that Levent was able to palm away before returning a punch which made contact with Arnold's cheek. Arnold then tried again but Levent managed to block these before he attempted to catch him with a kick. Levent stepped back away from it before jumping forward and landing multiple punches on Arnold before kneeing him in the stomach, the force instantly took his breath away. Dropping to his knees, Levent aimed another couple of punches that Arnold was able to block before Levent grabbed hold of him by the hair and connected with another two punches.

"You thought you stood a chance?" he raged as he before pulled Arnold to his feet, slamming his fist into his stomach, causing him to drop to the floor again. Arnold spat a mouthful of blood onto the floor as he stared down at the dirt beneath him.

Otto and the lion continued to exchange blows with one another, the lion managed to make contact with Otto's leg, causing him to let out a roar of pain. It took a swipe at his head, sending him crashing through the air and into the wall beside them. The lion was quickly over him and slammed its giant paws into his chest repeatedly before attempting to bite down on him. Otto grabbed hold of the spirit beast's jaws and held them tightly preventing it from biting down on him. Blood began pouring from his hands where the lion's teeth had pierced his skin.

Arnold couldn't pick himself up in time and Levent kicked him with tremendous force, catapulting him to the side. He was taking a hammering. Arnold had not laid a punch on Levent. He was not strong enough to beat him and didn't know whether or not he would be able to continue the fight. He began to glow and within a moment, his spirit beast had been summoned despite being weakened and unable to fly from the injury it had sustained from Otto. It stood in front of Arnold with one wing outstretched as though protecting him. Feeling a second wind, he brought himself back to his feet and he felt a surge of courage from within. He might not be as strong, but he was going to give Levent a good fight. He stood up straight, his face bloodied and bruised and braced himself for another round, his blue auro glowing around him. Levent grinned maniacally and removed his overcoat. He pulled out his dagger and readied his stance for Arnold.

A wave of panic overcame Arnold as he was without a weapon. He needed to think quickly before it was too late. He was about to lose; he couldn't take Levent on hand to hand and now he had his blade. Arnold had almost accepted defeat when his eagle stood in front of him and slammed its wing down to the ground. It looked across to the side of them as though trying to get his attention. Arnold followed the line of sight and saw the broken hilt from the macuahuitl. He was momentarily confused but suddenly clarity unclouded his mind and he understood what his spirit beast was guiding him to do.

"I've had enough now!" Levent screamed as he ran towards Arnold with his blade outstretched.

Arnold dived to his side and reached for macuahuitl hilt and focused, trying his hardest to keep his mind clear. His blue auro began to glow even brighter around him. Holding onto the hilt he pictured the macuahuitl in its full form and pure energy from the spirit world re-forged the blade exactly how it had been before. From its paddle-like shaft to the blades that ran around the outer edge, Arnold had a spirit wielded a weapon to defend himself.

Levent drew his blade towards Arnold, who swung his macuahuitl upwards with one hand and was able to parry the attack away. Arnold couldn't believe how light the blade was having grown used to the weight it was before. The pure spirit energy which was now flowing through the weapon made it almost weightless in comparison. He could feel the energy coursing through him, he felt on the edge of control but It was control non the less.

"You can spirit wield? You do surprise me. Still, the

result will be the same," Levent sneered. He jabbed forward with his blade, which Arnold parried with ease. He jabbed forward a couple of more times before speeding up and swinging a flurry of blows at Arnold which he was able to continue to deflect. Arnold could see Otto behind Levent holding the lion's jaws tightly as it was attempting to bite down on him. His arms were beginning to buckle from the prolonged grapple.

Levent came at Arnold again and the two of them began swinging their weapons against each other as they each tried to outdo the other. Arnold was able to move so much faster than he usually did, making his macahuitl so much easier to wield. The two of them slammed their weapons against each other and drew face to face. Arnold was focusing on keeping his spirit wielding energy up through his auro and Levent growled at Arnold with pure hatred. Arnold could see the lion's jaws getting closer to Otto and sensing he didn't have much time he went at Levent with a flurry of blows which Levent blocked. Each blow was knocking him back slightly further and Arnold quickly swung out his other arm making contact with Levent's face, the connection of which was so satisfying. He then hit his macuahuitl repeatedly against Levent's blade before suddenly spinning the other way and swinging the blade downwards towards his leg. Levent screamed as Arnold macuahuitl cut through the back of his achilles, forcing him to the floor.

The lion flinched as it shared Levent's pain. Sensing his opportunity, Otto pushed back against the lion forcefully and twisted its jaws. The lion attempted to fight back, but sensing the upper hand, Otto continued to twist the lion's jaws until it eventually cracked and dropped to the floor motionless.

"No, you can't do this!" Levent was as furious as ever as he fell to the floor, unable to balance with his leg injured. "I can't stop her. I can't take her dragon unless she is in this world! Sixteen years! It has taken me sixteen years!" Dropping his blade, Arnold quickly kicked it away from him before dropping to his knees, exhausted from the battle. "Go on, finish it. Have your revenge. It's over now."

Arnold moved in towards Levent with his macuahuitl above his head. He had wanted this revenge since the day Levent murdered his grandad.

"Death would be too kind," he sighed before slamming the hilt of his blade into the side of Levent's head with as much force he could muster, rendering him unconscious. He had won. He had defeated him. He had avenged his grandad.

Arnold stood over Levent's unconscious body and Otto limped across in his were-jaguar form. He did not appear aggressive and seemed to be more in control of what he was doing. He reached down and picked up Levent before throwing him over his shoulder. His leg was bleeding, but not as much as you would normally imagine as Arnold's spirit blade's raw energy had appeared to cauterise the wound upon contact. Otto began to leave the room and grumbled towards Arnold as an indication for him to follow. With Levent over his shoulder, the two of them began their journey to the surface. Arnold had succeeded in what they had set out to do. He had saved his friends and stopped Mayor Redburn's plan. They had also captured Levent, the person who had masterminded everything and manipulated everyone.

CHAPTER 25

Arnold and Otto left the coal mine side by side. Arnold immediately began looking around for Everett, George and Marrok so he could check that they all were ok. He swung around and could see George sat on the floor holding Marrok who looked pretty beaten up. Everett stood on the other side of Marrok, a blank look in her eyes.

"Is he ok?" Arnold called over to George.

"I think he'll be ok. He just needs patching up." George was channelling her auro onto Marrok, trying her hardest to ease his pain and make him a little more comfortable.

Everett saw that Otto was carrying Levent and looked over at a nearby tree before requesting that he take Levent over there and guard him until the others arrived. Otto obliged and carried the unconscious Levent to where he had been asked before shifting out of his were-jaguar form.

"You control Night-Sun now, Everett," Marrok explained, "You wield the dagger."

"I don't want to control him. Otto, are you ok?" Otto

looked disorientated as he came around from his transformation, a painful process; his bones were resetting into their natural position.

"I'll be ok, how is everyone else?"

"I think we're all ok." Arnold was glad to see everyone ok aside from some minor injuries. Everett became tearful and before she knew it, her eyes were filled with tears that she could not hold back any longer. "My spirit beast, is she gone?" Marrok shuffled up, so he was sitting rather than laid on the floor and took hold of Everett's hand to comfort her.

"I'm afraid so. I arrived too late. She was absorbed by the gateway and her spirit energy became part of it." He answered.

"So, I am a menial. I have no spirit beast anymore?" Everett looked dejected a wave of sadness overcoming her. She was grieving for her spirit beast, knowing that she would never see it again.

"I'm so sorry, Everett," George said trying to console her but to little effect. "If you hadn't saved mine-"

"Don't," Marrok cut her off. "You will torture yourself with what-ifs."

"Where is my dad? Did anyone see where he went?" Otto was referring to Mayor Redburn, who had bolted from the coal mine as the final confrontation was taking place.

"I don't know. We came up out of the mine and he was already gone. He was being manipulated this whole time, Otto. You can't be mad at him. He was doing what he thought he needed to, to save you." Marrok attempted to bargain with Otto, but his attempts fell on deaf ears.

"He chose to do what he did. He chose to control me. He chose to make me attack you all." Otto wasn't happy and he wanted to be the one that found him so he could let him know just how unhappy with him he was.

Across the field Arnold could see a group of people approaching, he knew from the animal hides they were wearing that they were the Almec. As they approached, Arnold wondered what they would want to do now that the crisis had been resolved. That Otto, or Night-Sun to them, was ok.

"Night-Sun, how are you feeling?" the leader asked as she dropped the hood of her coyote hide to her shoulders.

It took Otto a few moments to realise that she was talking to him; he was not used to going by that name. "Please call me Otto. I am ok, thanks. I don't know what to do now that my dad is not in control of me. What should I do with the blade?" he shrugged.

"This is still a difficult situation that you find yourself in. You see, you cannot hold the blade. To do so would risk your corruption worsening and possibly fully losing control of your humanity. Someone needs to look after that blade. May I recommend that we do this for you? Night-Sun, you are our deity and as such we are here to help you. Our culture exists to serve you." Otto felt taken aback by this as it was not what he had asked for, nor was it what he wanted.

"Does that mean I am stuck this way?" The leader of the Almac nodded.

"Yes, there is no way to reverse corruption; your souls are now intertwined." Otto was expecting to hear this, but he did not fully trust the Almec as he had only recently met them. He knew who he wanted to wield the blade that could potentially control him.

"Everett, I want you to hold on to that for me and protect it. It's hard to explain, but I felt like I could read you when you asked me to help against Levent. All I could see was kindness and selflessness and I know I can trust you with it."

Everett was taken aback at what had been asked of her; Otto had just trusted his life with her. But it did not feel like a burden. She had found that while holding the blade, her connection with Otto had gotten stronger and that she understood what his wants and wishes were without him needing to say a word. She felt like they were now linked together in the same way she had been to her spirit beast.

"I will. For you, Otto. I will never command you to do

anything again as long as I hold it. I promise you. You will not be a slave to this blade." Otto smiled at her, but Arnold could see that deep down he was saddened at learning that he was stuck this way for the rest of his life and that he would never be able to command his jaguar spirit beast.

"Does this make me your spirit beast?" Otto tried to make light of the situation in front of the audience around them.

"Weirdly, I guess so," Everett smiled.

"What are we going to do with him? George was referring to Levent who remained unconscious behind Otto.

"He is coming with me to the Chichen," Arnold explained. "I hope you will respect that? He murdered my grandad and he will face the consequences for that." Arnold was talking to the Almec, just in case they had any plans to take him for themselves.

"We will not interfere with your business, Arnold, should Night-Sun wish it." She looked across at Otto who looked nervous at the position he had been put in. Otto had harbored his own hatred for Levent as it was he who had created the artefact that had been used on his spirit beast; it was his actions that made him this way. He did, however, understand Arnold's viewpoint and did not want to go against his best friend ever again. "He needs to go to the Chichen. He needs to go with Arnold."

The woman looked disappointed by Otto's choice but none the less respected his wishes. She looked across at Levent and Arnold couldn't help but feel that there was something that she was not telling them. There was a pain in her eyes and a great sadness.

"Very well, we will leave him in your care." The woman lifted her coyote hide hood and turned to leave. "Marrok, are you coming?"

"Yes, mum." He struggled to his feet and dusted himself down before walking over to the Almec and readied himself to leave. "I guess I'll see you around."

"Thank you." Arnold knew if not for his help in the mine, the story may very well have been different.

They began to leave but not before the woman left Otto with some parting words. "If you ever need anything we will be there to help. You need to be wary of the Chichen. If they learn of you, they will try to catch you and they will want that blade. Everett you can't let that happen."

"I won't. There is one thing, though?" Everett began.

"What's your name?" Arnold finished.

The woman smiled at them all, the moonlight reflected off her face and illuminated her natural beauty. "Please, my name is Kaliska." She waved them goodbye and the Almec began to leave altogether. Before long, they had all disappeared into the darkness, their whereabouts now unknown. Arnold couldn't help but feel that they would still be around, to keep watch on Otto and try and maintain his safety. He wouldn't let anything come between Otto and himself again. He would also do his best to try and ensure no harm came to him, even though this put him in direct conflict with the Chichen.

"I promise to protect your secret Otto, no matter what happens with the Chichen."

"I know you will, mate. Now how are we going to get him across there?" Otto was referring to the Chichen in Oswald.

"I'm going to have to call my dad. He will have to bring the others, which means..."

"I need to leave and stay low for a while, just until the dust settles." Otto understood and he wasn't offended. His main worry right now was where his dad was. "I'm going to head home. Text me later. All of you." With this Otto left them at the coal mine with Levent.

Arnold pulled out his phone and rang his dad to explain what had happened.

CHAPTER 26

It was not long before Arnold's dad and some other Doyen's arrived to support them, Levent was taken to hospital while in custody. Arnold, Everett and George were escorted to the Chichen. Once there, they were expected to give a detailed account of what had happened that night. They had told them everything that had happened at the coal mine, but they omitted Otto, Mayor Redburn and the Almec being there, pinning everything on Levent. They explained that he had tried to use George's spirit beast to open a gateway, but they said they did not know why.

Arnold sat in the reception area of the Chichen, waiting for his dad to come and tell him what was to happen next. He stared down at the floor and for a moment contemplated lying down on it and having a little sleep. He was so tired. He heard a door open and he looked up to see George being escorted out of Mr. Whittaker's office by her dads. She cast him a smile and waved at him as they walked past and out of the door.

"Arnold, can you come in please." Arthur stood by Mr. Whittaker's office with his hand outstretched, directing him to come across. Arnold obliged and walked towards the office, wondering what they wished to discuss with him now.

"Please sit down, Ethon." Mr. Whittaker's well-spoken voice directed. "You have managed to capture a highly dangerous wanted man and bring him back to the Chichen. In doing so, you have proven your ability in combat as well as your aptitude. Not only but this I am led to believe that you were able to spirit wield a weapon while in combat against Levent. Is this all true?"

"I guess so." Arnold wanted to stay modest about his actions. He had done what he had set out to do. He had captured the man who had murdered his grandad in front of him.

"Your actions have brought great honour to this Chichen. Your grandad would be proud." Arnold felt conflicted, his grandad would be proud. However, Mr. Whittaker was unaware of his grandad's affiliation with the Almec. Or that deep down, his grandad was not fully on board with the Chichen and their ways.

"Where is Levent? What will happen to him?" Having not seen him since the Doyen's arrived, he was curious about his whereabouts and what they were going to do with him.

"He will be detained in London, at the maximum-security prison Glyckeria. He will remain under constant supervision there."

"And his blade?" asked Arnold.

Mr. Whittaker shuffled some papers on his desk before answering. "Why, the Chichen will keep hold of it to stop it falling into anyone else's hands." His response was quick and short, he looked unhappy that Arnold was questioning him. "There is something that I would like you to see. If you would follow your dad, I believe he would like to explain this next part to you." He gestured to Arthur for him to take over at this point.

"Come on son, this way."

Arnold followed his dad, to the elevator that sat in the centre of the Chichen. The last time Arnold had entered the elevator, he had undertaken his Ch 'ahb' which was his initiation. To set him on the path he needed to follow to become a Doyen. The experience had felt like a dream. He did remember how nervous he had been and how intimidating and scary it had been. His dad sensed his nervousness and smiled at him in an attempt to ease his anxieties.

"Don't worry, its nothing like the Ch 'ahb'," he laughed, trying to make light of the situation. Pressing the button to the lift, it illuminated straight away and within a few seconds the doors opened and the two of them entered.

"What about Otto, Dad? We can't let anyone know about him." Arnold hadn't had the chance to speak with him about his friend, his dad knew that Otto was Night-Sun.

"I won't say a word as long as he is in control. I won't have any choice otherwise, Arnold. I can't let anybody get hurt."

"I understand. Thanks, Dad. Now, where is it you are taking me?" He had seen his dad press one of the four buttons in the elevator. Each one had a different symbol on that Arnold did not understand. The last time he had been in here, his dad had pressed the very bottom symbol and this time he had touched the second one.

"I want to give you a bit more insight into your spirit beast, into your eagle. I am taking you to an area where you now have permitted access, as you have captured a highly dangerous criminal and proven yourself to the Chichen."

Arnold's eyes lit up in excitement. He felt he knew what was coming but wanted to seek assurances that his idea was correct. "Am I about to receive my first ranking?"

His dad smiled and nodded at Arnold as the elevator opened to reveal a large armory. There were ancient weapons and armour lined up on each side of the room, ranging from ancient and old fashioned to the more modern interpretations. There were many sets of ancient armour, each crafted from unique materials. It was truly mesmerising for Arnold who could not believe the ancient relics that lay hidden on this floor. They walked down the centre of the long room until his dad stopped.

"As you are aware, there are many ranks within the Chichen and currently I carry the rank of Doyen, which translates as 'the protector'. I wanted to show you something incredible, given what your spirit beast is and what Otto's was before his transformation." He pressed the button of a small remote that he had picked up and two sets of armour lit up on the opposite side of the room to them. "Look at the armour and tell me - what do you see?" Arnold began to examine the two sets of armour. The one on the left was the hide of a jaguar, he could tell by the markings and the similar shape of the headpiece to Otto's spirit beast. The one on the right was adorned with perfectly placed feathers. Parts of the chain mail armour could be seen underneath and it looked like finely polished gold that bound the breastplate together. The feathers looked familiar to Arnold and it did not take him long for him to recognise them as being the same type of feathers that his spirit beast had. Arnold's eyes shone in the light as he stood in awe of the ancient sets of armour that stood before him encased in a large glass container. Each set of armour had individual lights fitted in each cabinet shining a light on the magnificent detail, showcasing the mastery and craft that had gone into making them.

"An eagle and a jaguar?" Arnold was confident of his guess. The patterns on the materials were too similar for him to be wrong.

"That's right," Arthur responded a smile on his face at Arnold's reaction to seeing the armour. It took him back to when Arnold was a small child, seeing his face light up when he saw the presents that Father Christmas had left him on Christmas morning. He looked at his son with so much pride at what he had been able to achieve in first protecting his friends and then capturing Levent. It was something that the

Doyens had not been able to accomplish since he escaped. "You have shown a tremendous amount of bravery in what you have achieved Arnold. I am so incredibly proud of you. You have protected those that needed your help without hesitation and demonstrated courage and strength beyond your years. As well as this, you have captured an incredibly powerful foe who had caused us great pain and anguish and not allowed your anger to consume you. You accepted the guidance of your spirit beast and have proven yourself." His dad pressed another button on the remote he was holding and the glass casing opened on the eagle armour. "This is yours now, son. You need to get dressed and then I will take you to the ceremonial chamber."

Arnold picked up the armour and was surprised at how light it was. "What's going to happen?" he asked.

"You will receive your rank. I'll wait for you at the elevator."

Arthur walked over to the elevator and walked in, shutting the doors behind him. "I'll come and get you when you are ready," he called as the elevator doors closed. Arthur went to the changing rooms and got dressed into his green ceremonial robes before entering the elevator once more where he stopped on the second floor to collect Arnold. At this point, Arthur couldn't tell who was more nervous - his son or himself. The doors opened and stood there was an uncomfortable-looking Arnold, who had managed to figure out how to put the set of armour on.

"It feels itchy," he said as he pulled at the collar. Arthur laughed and stepped to the side to allow Arnold in.

"That's because it hasn't been worn in over two hundred years." The doors shut and Arthur pressed to go down to the base floor. It was the ceremonial chamber where Arnold had completed his Ch'ahb'. This time it was better lit and he could see the solid stone walls that had been untouched since the Chichen had been built. He recognised the stone casket in the centre of the room and he knew the Elder that stood just in front of it, he was also dressed in his ceremonial robes. It was Mr Whittaker. Arnold didn't recognise some of the other men and women that stood around the room in different coloured ceremonial robes. By looking at the various symbols on each person's robe, he quickly deduced that they were representatives of Chichen's from different parts of the country.

"Go on, son." Arthur prompted him to step forward into the ceremonial chamber. Arnold suddenly felt pressure which he was not expecting because of the impressive number of people within the room. Arnold was baffled at how they had all got there so soon. However, he was impressed at them coming to see him too. This was something that Arnold could have never imagined in his wildest dreams.

"Step forward, Arnold Ethon." Mr. Whittaker beckoned him to move further forward and stand in front of him. Arnold followed the instructions and stepped forward. He was amazed at how easy he found it to manoeuvre in his armour. It felt as though it was weightless, as light as a feather almost. He stopped and stood directly in front of Mr. Whittaker, who began to address the room.

"Arnold Ethon has proven himself in his ability to protect others. He has also proven himself in battle as well as demonstrating the rarest of abilities of spirit wielding. His power runs through his bloodline. With his spirit beast, he has shown he has a commitment to the ways passed down in the Chichen. It is unheard of for someone of his years to be able to demonstrate the skill that he has consistently shown. He stands before you in armour not worn for two hundred years. The last person who wore that armour also had an eagle for their spirit beast. Arnold, this armour was crafted over a millennia ago. It is ancient and it is imbued with incredible power. When wearing this armour in training or battle your abilities to spirit wield as well as your mastery with your spirit beast will become less strenuous on your body. It will allow you a greater connection with your auro."

"Thank you." Arnold nodded his head to Mr. Whittaker in his appreciation for the ancient armour that he had just received. It all seemed so surreal that he felt he should pinch himself. He was stood in a room full of Elders from across the country having just captured Levent and adorned in armour made out of eagle feathers.

"You are not of an age where I can grant you the rank of Doyen; however, I do have the authority to give you an incredible rank which I now have the pleasure of granting you. This rank within the Chichen is rare and it is a testament to the skills you have shown with your mind, body and spirit. It is a rank that I do not doubt you will bring great honour to during your time in the Chichen." Arnold's heart was pumping. He felt he might faint at any point because of how fast it was pumping his blood around his body. He waited nervously through the moments of silence while waiting to hear what his rank would be. "I now grant you the rank of Eagle Warrior."

He had his rank, he had his role within the Chichen and he felt truly honoured to be accepted in this way. He turned to face the room of Elders who had begun clapping and applauding and could see his dad at the back of the room, clapping the hardest and the loudest. His eyes were filled with tears at his son's momentous achievement. Arnold felt delighted to see how proud his dad looked, but it did not stop the conflict that Arnold now felt in his heart.

His conflict arose from knowing the truth. His Grandad as an Elder of the Chichen had been working with the Almec. He may have even held rank with them. The Chichen and the Almec held different rules and views on how spirit beasts should be wielded and how auros should be channeled. The two of them had been opposed to each other throughout history. The Almec was thought not to exist anymore, but Arnold knew different. Not only this, he had worked with them to capture Levent. As he left the ceremonial chamber, he could not help but feel that soon he was going to have to make a choice.

The Chichen or the Almec.

CHAPTER 27

Far within the darkness that engulfed the coal mines, nothing could be heard. Not an animal or nature. There was no wind blowing down the tunnels nor the echoing sounds that might have travelled down from outside. All that existed within these tunnels now was darkness.

The lion spirit beast that had been slain by Otto lay motionless on the ground. A wind appeared to ruffle the beast's fur the force that was creating this movement was unnatural and gradually getting more powerful. The energy within the room began to rise. The lion slowly began to slide along the floor toward the point where the force was coming from. The lion raised into the air and disappeared as it was absorbed in the same manner that Everett's boar had been when Levent had sacrificed it to the gateway. The chamber began to shake violently as the energy levels continued to rise before a distorted portal appeared, much larger than the one that Levent had used. The gateway had opened but nobody was there to witness it. The power was immense. The chamber continued to shake with sections of the mine beginning to crumble.

From within the gateway a figure could be seen. It moved closer towards the distorted opening, illuminating the room. It leaned forward and a hand emerged from within the portal. The fingers moving as it tested what the area felt like. A foot then emerged from the gateway followed by the other as the figure fully emerged.

Taking a huge gulp of the thin air the woman wondered where she was. She did not care as she had finally escaped from the spirit world.

She smiled as she summoned her powerful spirit beast to guide her from this dark place. Her beauty became distorted as her sinister expression was revealed. She had waited for this moment for a very long time indeed. She had escaped the prison where she had been held for over fourty years.

She was free and ready for her revenge.

Arnold and his friends will return in
The War Of The Roses

ABOUT THE AUTHOR

A.P Beswick hails from a small town in the north west of England named Oswaldtwistle. He is married to his wife Sarah and has three children Libbi, Connor and Etta. As well as being an author A.P Beswick is also a registered mental health nurse, specilising in complex learning disabilities.

Stay up to date with A.P Beswick's other titles in development by joining his newsletter on www.apbeswick.com

Printed in Great Britain
by Amazon

68999553R00139